# The Cursed Shore

by

Ellen Hiller

Published by New Generation Publishing in 2020

Copyright © Ellen Hiller 2020

First Edition

The author asserts the moral right under the Copyright, Designs and Patents Act 1988 to be identified as the author of this work.

All Rights reserved. No part of this publication may be reproduced, stored in a retrieval system or transmitted, in any form or by any means without the prior consent of the author, nor be otherwise circulated in any form of binding or cover other than that which it is published and without a similar condition being imposed on the subsequent purchaser.

ISBN 978-1-80031-903-5

**www.newgeneration-publishing.com**

New Generation Publishing

# The BookChallenge
WHAT'S YOUR STORY?

This book was shortlisted in the Pen to Print Book Challenge Competition and has been produced by The London Borough of Barking and Dagenham Library Service - Pen to Print Creative Writing Programme. This is supported with National Portfolio Organisation funding from Arts Council, England.

*Pen to* Print
WHAT'S YOUR STORY?

Connect with Pen to Print
Email: pentoprint@lbbd.gov.uk
Web: pentoprint.org

Supported using public funding by
**ARTS COUNCIL ENGLAND**

**Barking & Dagenham**

*January 25th, 1796, Aglets Cove, Cornwall*

The bitter wind whipped across the surface of the sea, slashing into their already numb faces as if to flay them alive. Harsh as it was, it was no more than they had suffered before, and the prize was always worth one night of agony on the storm-battered shoreline.

Jacob stood third inline of the short chain of men and women leading to the beach, already up to his waist in the freezing winter sea. Jacob reached out to take another large oilskin-covered barrel from the man in front. It was heavy to lift, what with his back, wracked in pain and threatening to seize up altogether. However, big, and heavy was worth more, it meant a substantial prize for one night's work. No matter what the elements threw at them, the prize was always worth it.

Jacob yelled a warning about the weight of the barrel to the man behind him but the howling wind blew the words from his lips and they went unheard. He shrugged an apology as the man fumbled the casket and almost lost his footing. In the relentless wind, and with the huge waves crashing like thunder against the rocks of the cove, there was no choice but to work in silence as they emptied the small boat of its precious cargo of brandy and tea.

The receding tide tugged at the boat, making Jacob and the whole line move a step further into the surf. Despite already being drenched in rain and seawater, that extra step forwards made Jacob gasp anew as the intense cold moved up his body and found new flesh to chill. Determined to ignore the discomfort, he pushed on, fighting against the surge of the sea, the dragging of the current around his legs and the treacherous sand shifting beneath his feet.

Jacob received the next barrel with a grimace and passed it on. If he'd counted right, there was only three more to go, and then they'd be done. After that, it was just a quick run along the cliff path and back home to the warmth and comfort of Beth's arms and the comforting sounds of the little ones sleeping in their cots.

As he forced his arms up to take the last barrel, the resounding crack of a musket broke the air like thunder. Jacob instinctively let go of the barrel and watched it drop into the water and bob away on the ebbing tide with a sinking heart. Then he turned around to face the line of Revenue men that he knew would be waiting for them on the beach. Their reloaded guns were pointing at himself and the rest of the smugglers.

\*\*\*

# CHAPTER 1

June 1st, 2019, Aglets Cove, Cornwall

Steven Pearn stood at the door and studied the keys in his hands. They were nan's keys, not his. They felt as strange and intrusive in his hand as he did, standing under her porch. His porch now. He hesitated, knowing that when he opened the door, the cottage would be empty. There would be no welcoming hugs or rough kisses on his cheek to wipe away, no smell of freshly baked cakes and furniture polish. There would be no Nan. He took a deep breath and opened the door at last, then stepped into what had always been his favourite place in the whole world.

The cottage still smelled of his childhood memories and the holidays he had spent there, a mixture of cakes and lavender, and the underlying muskiness of the granite rock the cottage had been built from an age ago. Even though the place had been empty for over a month now, Steven was pleased that, instead of the expected cold emptiness, it was still warm and homely. There was no chill or damp from the stone walls, just a soothing coolness that enveloped him and welcomed him to his new home.

He threw the keys into the little pottery bowl on the coffee table, just as Nan had always done, and sat down on the flowery sofa. The springs groaned and sagged a little under him, even though he carried little in the way of excess weight. Good, an excuse to get rid of the old thing he thought. Not that he needed an excuse, he sighed as he looked around at the small army of ornaments that covered the shelves, windowsills, and the mantelpiece. The clutter was a part of Nan and throwing her old things out was going to be hard.

Steven checked his watch; it was still early, so he decided to leave the suitcases where they were and head down to the little café on the seafront for some breakfast. He smiled to himself, knowing it was just an excuse to visit the beach. Then couldn't suppress the laugh that followed. He could visit the beach anytime he wanted now. He lived here, here in Aglets Cove, the place of his childhood holidays and long weekend escapes from the city. No need to escape now, he could live the life he always dreamed of. Nothing this good had ever happened to him before, this was a new life that he couldn't wait to start.

The short drive to the beach was picturesque. Summer had found Cornwall at last, and everything was a vibrant green with sharp contrasts between the bright sunlight and the shade of the trees. Steven drank it all in with an eager thirst as he drove along the coast road.

As he rounded the last bend in the lane that would take him past the old church and onto the seafront, Steven was met with the sight of a full walking funeral procession coming towards him.

'Oh, of course,' he said to himself as he remembered Sandra telling him that old miss Marjory had died this week. This must be her funeral. He swerved into a small layby, got out of the car, and stood; head bowed in respect as they carried the coffin past him. One by one, the villagers ambled past, some recognising him and offering condolences on his own loss, and all of them keeping time with the tolling of the church bell.

The procession seemed to take forever to pass. Steven didn't realise the woman was so popular, what with her reputation for being an evil old witch and all. He smiled sympathetically and nodded at Miss Doryty, Marjory's sister, who was at the back of the procession, walking slowly, a heavy black lace veil obscuring her face.

*The Cursed Shore*

Assuming that his duty of respect was done Steven turned to open the car door, only to be horrified when Miss Doryty stopped to talk to him.

'My, what a handsome young man you have grown into, young Steven,' she said as she reached up to ruffle his hair as if he was still a small child and Steven winced at the sharp tug when one of her many elaborate rings got caught. Miss Doryty tugged her hand free and smiled at him through the veil as if she had not noticed his discomfort then carried on walking down the lane towards the church.

Steven, relieved to escape the social awkwardness of the situation, climbed back into his car and drove on past the row of quaint fishermen's cottages to the seafront with its kitsch souvenir shops. The café hadn't opened yet, so Steven drove straight into the cove car park and wasted no time in whisking off his shoes and socks and sinking his feet into the deep fine sand of the beach.

Aglets Cove was a narrow stretch of beach bordered on one side by a low cliff and the other by a dark rocky outcrop into which a set of stone steps had been carved centuries before. They were ancient and worn with no sides or handrail to stop you from falling off the side and onto the rocks, and the lower steps, which were covered at high tide, were slippery with seaweed and treacherous to climb. Still, for the experienced walker, they provided a quick way to get up to the coastal path which the ramblers and locals loved. Sensible families and an adult Steven entered via the car park at the side of the cliff.

As a child, Steven would scamper up and down those steps before running barefoot along the costal path to where it sloped down at the end of his grandmother's lane. Until one day, the reckless child grew up and grew tired of scraped shins and nettle stung feet. Now he was happy to take the longer route and drive there.

Walking along the beach, Steven felt a sense of a sense of coming home, of being exactly where he was meant to be. Even though he visited his nan regularly, especially since he started to get to know Sandra, the barmaid from the smuggler's inn. He always missed the cove when he was away from it and was never happier than when he returned.

Today was different though, today he had become a resident; he didn't have to go home at the end of the weekend or the end of the holiday, he was here to stay. He belonged.

After the initial excitement of being at the seaside wore off, he realised something was not quite right this morning. A strange smell was wafting over on top of the sea breeze, and it was quite unpleasant. Steven scanned the beach expecting to see a buzzing of flies and the rotting remains of a picnic nearby. It was immaculate as usual, he looked further down the cove and spotted something on the far side that the local gulls were extremely interested in and he trudged through the fine sand to investigate.

The closer Steven got to the seagulls, the more abhorrent the smell became until he had to cover his nose and mouth with his hand in order to take another step. The object the seagulls surrounded was bigger than he had first thought and there were several seagulls pecking at it and squabbling with each other to get closer. Despite the gulls obscuring most of the view, there was no mistaking the half skeletal hand that jutted out to the side of the object.

'Well, shit!' Steven said to the universe who dared to dump this obscene object onto his childhood memories. He pulled his phone out from his pocket and called the police.

The wait for the police seemed to last forever and morbid curiosity took over his revulsion, he crept forwards a few paces, much to the gull's distaste as they flew squawking around him. He gave the body a quick look. The arms and legs were mostly skeletal with strips of pale puffy flesh hanging from the bones; this was being diminished at an alarming rate by the birds. There were enough bits of

*The Cursed Shore*

clothing to hide the victim's decency but not enough to hide what looked like bruising around the tops of the arms where there was still puffy flesh enough to see, and on one of the wrists which was still intact, there was a thin line of dark blue bruising. Steven took an unconscious step back. Was he looking at a murder victim? To him it looked as if the poor person had been restrained at some point before his death.

The gulls were bored with Steven's intrusion now and pushed past him to get to the body, causing a fresh waft of death and decay to come up and assault him. He staggered back, gagging, and allowed them to obscure the view once more. He could taste the foulness now as well as smell it. He kept walking backwards, unable to turn away from the grotesque spectacle he didn't want to see, transfixed even when he was far enough away that he couldn't make out the shape of the body anymore.

The tide was coming in again and small waves were creeping up the beach, splashing his feet, and wetting his trousers, but he didn't notice them, he was unable to look away from the corpse but still wanted to get as far away as possible from it. As he neared the cliff, he could hear the police car coming down the lane and into the car park at last and he began to relax slightly. Turning, he tripped over a length of rusty chain that was lying close to the edge of the cliff wall. He reached out to steady himself as a wave of dizziness washed over him, and he grabbed hold of the rusted iron mooring ring that was embedded in the cliff there to steady himself.

As soon as his fingers brushed against the metal, it was like touching an electric current. He tried to snatch his hand away, but it was impossible, it drew him in and held him fast. The sky became dark as night and somehow, he now stood in the middle of a brutal winters storm.

A howling wind buffeted him as he shivered, waist high in rapidly rising freezing cold water. He struggled to move but found that he was now chained fast to the mooring ring. And he wasn't alone. There were others chained as well, and they screamed and cursed and cried alongside him. All, like him, were frantically pulling against the chains that would not give.

A large wave crashed against them all sending a surge of water over their heads. Steven lost his footing for a moment and would have gone under if it were it not for the chains and crush of bodies around him keeping him upright. He spluttered and choked on the seawater and continued to fight the chains.

Something inside his mind kept telling him that this wasn't happening, it was all wrong and he shouldn't be here. He knew he couldn't really be experiencing this; it was obviously a nightmare that would end with him safely tucked up in bed. But it felt so real, it terrified him, and he was so cold, a vicious cold that sawed through his flesh to reach his bones. Steven was shivering violently, his teeth chattering hard enough to break, and for some reason he was seething with anger.

The water was past his chest now and reaching up his neck, each new wave sent it splashing into his face up his nose into his ears. He wondered, with a mind that wasn't his own, if it would be better to breathe it in, to end it now, rather than fight to the inevitable end. However, you can never underestimate the powerful need to survive, so instead, he spat the seawater out and gasped in air whenever there was a chance.

Another large wave crashed against him, higher this time, and his fellow captives grew silent now as each man and woman succumbed to the sea or the cold, hanging listlessly on their chains, heads dropping into the water that had claimed them. He was still fighting on though, his height giving him an advantage on the others. Adding to his terror, he realised that he was now alone, death had released the others from their suffering, but his torture continued. His rage increased with the injustice that had brought him to this end.

*The Cursed Shore*

A name came with that rage and he roared it with his last breath as the seawater closed over his face and forced its way into his mouth.

'Trevan!'

Steven fell back onto the sand, his head pounding, gasping air into his aching lungs. As his blurred vision came into focus, he saw that the figure of a police officer was looming over him.

'You okay, sir?' the constable asked, looking at Steven as if he had just grown a second head. Steven managed to mumble some half-audible words of reassurance and pointed to where the body lay across the beach. The police officer nodded sympathetically and briskly helped Steven to his feet then turned to leave, pausing for a moment to call over his shoulder, 'The way you called me, sounded a bit weird like. Are you sure you are okay?'

Steven could only shrug and busy himself with standing upright and brushing the sand from his trousers, his mind was still reeling with what he had experienced, a hallucination perhaps, or perhaps he had fainted and then dreamed the whole thing. Luckily, the police officer was more interested in joining his colleagues at the rotting corpse than listening to his answer and had already resumed his ungainly march through the sand towards it.

As Steven made his way swiftly back to the car park, he desperately hoped that no one else had noticed his 'moment' as he rushed to get to get off of the beach. Then he caught sight of old Miss Doryty, no doubt on her way back from the funeral, watching him from the cliff path. He gave her a feeble, embarrassed, wave and scuttled to the relatively safety of his car.

He decided to give breakfast a miss this morning and drove back towards the sanctity of his cottage, the car window wide open as he gulped in as much fresh air as he could.

Back at his Nan's cottage, Steven stripped off his clothes and headed to the shower. So much for his first day in Aglets Cove, he thought. He wondered how much scrubbing it would take to remove the smell of death and if maybe, he should burn the clothes.

There was of course one small silver lining to the morning's events. Tomorrow he started working full time as a journalist for the *West Coast Recorder*. He had worked for them on a freelance basis for some time, chasing up stories in the city that might be of interest to the locals. Now he lived here he was going to be a proper member of staff; with paid holidays and sick pay and all the benefits he had missed whilst self-employed. What a way to start his new position, he was sure they would love a first-hand account of the body on the beach.

He stuck his tongue in the flow of water and considered gargling bleach to remove the taste that still lingered there, mmm first-hand account, wasn't he the lucky one?

# CHAPTER 2

Police Constable Andrew Trevan stood next to the rotting corpse on the beach and tried not to inhale too deeply. Luckily, it wasn't his job to look for signs of foul play today so he didn't have to get any closer than he was already, and anyway, he knew there would be no evidence on the body. Trevan stepped back and let the other two officers retch as they turned the corpse on its side looking for suspicious injuries. He turned his back on the corpse and stood to attention, trying to maintain a professional detachment in case anyone was watching them, he didn't need to scan the cliffs, but it gave him something else to focus his attention on.

As the body was turned, fresh corpse juice leaked out from its numerous holes and what was left of the mouth. With it, a more intense smell of rotting flesh wafted up towards them.

Andrew decided to take a couple more steps backwards. Having to maintain a professional image in a situation like this was bad enough but maintaining his dignity was going to be a lot harder if he retched up all over the scene of crime. He couldn't help a smirk though as one of the other officers turned and lost his breakfast on the sands, even though it just made his own nausea worse.

The remaining officer let the body flop ungracefully back to its previous position where it oozed silently. Whilst avoiding the whole pulpy mess that had once been the man's face, Andrew gave a cursory glance at the body, noting the ring of bruising around the wrists. It was very apparent to all who saw it that the man must have been restrained before his death. He would have to have a chat with the pathologist about that once the body was sent off for a closer inspection. He grimaced at the thought. His job was more boring paperwork than he had anticipated when joining the force, but he would take a mountain of paperwork over examining that rotten wreck of a body any day.

Not soon enough, the van arrived in the car park with a new team to gag as they bagged the body up and carted it off, he was grateful they didn't ask for help. Once the body was whisked away, he joined the group who were scouring the beach for evidence, or missing body bits, it was a fruitless search and soon enough the beach was declared clean and he was free to return to the station.

Once in the sanctity of the car park, he took a moment to breathe in fresh air that wasn't contaminated with death as he kicked the sand off of his boots before climbing back into the squad car and shuddering. It was not only because of the thing that used to be a man that he had been forced to witness, having to spend any amount of time on that beach was especially traumatic for him, too many connections, and too many memories.

He thought about the man who had reported the body and had then fainted, and smiled sympathetically. Strange how the guy knew his name though, he was sure he didn't know him. Maybe the dispatcher told him who to expect, yeah probably that he thought as he turned on the ignition and drove back to the station.

# CHAPTER 3

A day later and Simon Dyer shivered as he sat waxing his new surfboard in the car park next to Aglets Cove beach. It was early; the sun had barely risen, but the surf was good, and there were no tourists about; what with yesterday's body and all. He grimaced as he ducked under the yellow warning tape to get into the cove, but he was reasonably certain the beach had had a good clean up and he wouldn't encounter any missing body parts in the water. At least the tape would keep the tourists away, so no spectators. Usually he didn't mind an audience, in fact he quite enjoyed it, but today was his first day with a new board and at a new beach. He wanted to make sure he had both mastered before he risked making a fool of himself in public.

Standing on the shoreline, the wind whipping through his curly ginger hair and the salt spray stinging his freckled face, Simon studied the sea. It was a little rough out there but nothing he hadn't handled before. A blast of cold wind buffeted against him and he thought of Jenny still snuggled up in bed back at their apartment and for a moment was almost tempted to join her. But the pull of the sea was too strong, it always had been, it always came first. He zipped his dry suit up to his chin, grabbed the luminous green board and started to paddle out to sea.

Surfing had been Simon's life since his mother had bought him his first body board at the age of five. His family lived in Devon, a little way outside of the Cornish border, so he had never been far from a good surfing beach. Even so, he still spent all his holidays in apartments at various surfing locations around the world. Some thought he was obsessed, but he didn't care. Never a moment missed, he surfed at the weekends and every holiday, summer or winter. Even some days after work he would sling the board in the back of the van and head off to some lonely beach, surfing long into the night. It was all he lived for.

There were only a few beaches around the south-west coast Simon had never surfed from, some because they were simply dull and full of newbie surfers getting in the way, and some because of the rocks hidden deceptively below the water line. He loved surfing, but not enough to die for it.

Then there was this one, Aglets Cove 'the cursed shore' as his father called it. Simon's father, who had grown up in the area, had always told him that he should never, under any circumstance, visit the place. There was never an explanation given and as a youngster, Simon was happy to obey his father's wishes without question. This all seemed so silly now as he sat on the board paddling out past the rocks. Perhaps his father had been worried about his safety; surfing this beach was for experts only. Simon, however, was now considered quite the expert and with the trophies to prove it. He knew he could surf it with ease, and a little thrill of rebellion shot through him when at last he reached the spot he had been aiming for.

Looking around at the rising surf, he was certain he would be able to catch all the best waves from here. He shivered again as a weird vibration tingled through his body and he wondered if he wasn't coming down with something nasty. It hadn't been this cold when he left the apartment before dawn and now the sun was up and the sky was cloudless, not to mention his dry suit was zipped up to his neck. He should be feeling totally snug.

The sudden screech of a seagull, its cries quickly taken up by several others, caused Simon to look over to his left. The sky there had darkened, and banks of dark blue and grey clouds were rolling in fast, hiding the sun until the

*The Cursed Shore*

whole area was engulfed in an eerie twilight. The wind blew stronger whipping the surrounding waves into a frenzy. He began to feel uneasy; he was a good swimmer and was always at home in the water, but he was wise enough to know how deadly it could suddenly become. Always respect the weather and its effect on the sea he had been taught, never think you can get the better of it.

He sat astride the board weighing up the odds, should he carry on and see what occurred? He could wait on the beach for it to pass over or give up now, go home, and finish the morning snuggled up in bed with the lovely Jenny. It was tempting, but so was having this new place to surf to himself, or so he had thought. Back on the shoreline, he glimpsed movement on the beach; he turned his board for a better look. Yes, there were people there, a small group standing together by the cliffs, looking out to sea.

Simon looked over his shoulder following their gaze, trying to see what they were watching, but there was nothing out there but blue grey sea. Surely, they were not watching him. Maybe they were waiting to watch him surf, he wondered. The showman that lived constantly inside him refused to disappoint a willing crowd and without a second thought of the weather he paddled the board into the next wave and expertly jumped to his feet. Simon rode into it, the wild wind pulling at his hair, his arms outstretched, and knees bent, perfectly balanced. He rode the wave with ease, this is what life was for, this and the booze and the girls of course.

A low rumbling filled the heavy sky, thunder? Surely not, the forecast hadn't mentioned anything like it, yet there it was again, a low rumble echoing off the cliffs and alongside it the wind making a strange wailing sound as it echoed around the cove. The wind blew stronger, and the clouds darkened the sky enough to resemble an eerie twilight as Simon rode his wave closer to the shore anxious now to end the exhibition.

The group on the beach continued to watch him, and a sense of unease came over him as he came closer to them, they appeared strange, unnatural, and the closer he got the stranger they seemed. They were dressed all wrong, not the sort of clothes you wore on a beach holiday, and why were they still there when there was a storm brewing? Simon could now see that it was not only their dress sense that did not fit, they were generally unkempt, as if they had all just woken from a bad night's sleep.

It just didn't make sense.

Closer now and Simon noticed their movements, also wrong, people didn't move like that, and they were moving towards him, right up to the water's edge and they were wet, it wasn't even raining yet, but they were drenched and dripping. The wave that brought him close to the shoreline had dispersed and Simon sat on the board and nervously started to hand paddle it back away from the beach. He was about a hundred yards out now, and despite the cold bite of the sea, he was determined not to come any closer until they were all gone.

His stomach knotted tight as he watched them, they were smiling and laughing with wide gaping mouths, pointing at him. He spun around, hoping to see something else there, hoping once again not to be the object of their attention, but he was alone.

He looked back again and gasped in horror as his stomach muscles cramped involuntarily, he didn't want to see it, but his eyes held fast, a shape in the water, in front of his board, then a hand, a pale deathly white hand grabbed the board. It was grotesque with flesh peeling from the fingers and maggots squirming in the tattered wounds. His first thought was that it was part of yesterday's murder victim that had been detached and he tried not to puke as he kicked at it in the hope of sending it on its way again. But the hand did not budge, in fact its fingers moved and griped the board even tighter.

*The Cursed Shore*

Simon shrieked in panic, what the hell was happening here? Worse still, why was it happening to him? He had never felt so alone or so frightened as he waited, trembling, for the rest of the body to emerge from the water. He did not want to think what would happen when it did. He hoped it was some kind of joke, a prank, the locals trying to scare him perhaps, but he knew in his heart it was too much to hope for. While he watched the pale hand, transfixed, waiting, gut clenched, full of dread, he was grabbed from behind by something, or someone pulling him with great strength away from his board.

Simon struggled as hard as he could and lashed out as he spun round in the water, trying to fight an assailant he could not see. Something grabbed hold of his legs; he tried to kick against it but could not move. No matter how hard he fought, every struggle was met with a tighter hold. Before he was pulled beneath the waves, he called out, desperately hoping someone else would be around at this hour, someone to save him from this nightmare, but he knew there was no one who could help. His screams turned to gurgles as the sea flowed unrelenting down his throat and into his burning lungs. The sea closed in over him and still he continued to lash out without managing to connect to anything of substance. Then there was nothing to fight with, his strength had gone and there was no air to replenish it. His last thoughts were of his father's warning words: *beware of the cursed shore*. As his burning vision slowly turned to darkness, he finally gave up the fight.

The impending storm never happened and the arms that had held him down were no longer there. The sky cleared, and the sun shone brightly once more, warming the sea and sand. The beach was empty, the sea was calm again, and a luminous green surfboard floated slowly towards the beach, gently guided by the small lapping waves, and a boy's lifeless body drifted on the whim of the tide.

# CHAPTER 4

As the morning sun crept over his eyes, Steven opened them and squinted at the brightness. He yawned and rubbed at his numb face, still groggy from a fitful night's sleep full of menacing faces and violent storms, stormy seas, and somewhere in the background, he was sure he heard the crack of gunfire. He contemplated going back to sleep in search of more pleasant dreams and snuggled back into the duvet, turned his back to the sun and tried to relax. However, his brain would not cooperate and refused to switch off. He turned over, thumped his pillow a few times and tried to force himself to relax, it didn't work. This was pointless he thought and sighed as he kicked off the covers and gave up. Anyway, he needed to get up and get ready for the first day of his new job this morning, so he might as well start now.

He made the effort to get out of bed and carefully navigated his way down the steep stairs and headed to the kitchen. A large mug of coffee and a croissant later and all was right with the world again. The first morning in his new home he thought, smiling to himself. He stretched feeling energised once more; he was ready to start the new day. He hoped it wouldn't be as dramatic as yesterday.

As he ate, Steven turned on the TV to catch the local news and wasn't surprised to find it all about the body on the beach. So, the cause of death had been confirmed as drowning, no surprise there. They reported that the body had suffered some bruising prior to death, which may have been caused by a fall from the cliffs onto the rocks before being swept out to sea. It could have been drifting on the

*The Cursed Shore*

tides for some time before the sea eventually brought it into Aglets Cove. Steven took a large swig of coffee and tried not to remember the smell of the rotting corpse. He did however remember the bruising around the corpse's wrist, this surely was not consistent with a fall, but it was not mentioned at all, he guessed that it was being kept quiet while they investigated the matter. He was no police officer, but he was positive that this was more than a simple accidental death.

The person on the TV then moved on to the history of the cove and how there had been bodies washed up here before, the last time being over fifty years ago. Steven placed his mug down and stared at the TV, why did he never hear of this before? He wondered if maybe the placing of the cove made it easier for something the size and shape of a body to wash up into. The tide did have a way of pushing some things into some coves and beaches and not others. A fact proved when in 1997 a ship was hit by a freak wave and lost containers containing Lego pieces overboard. Since then, Lego pieces had been continually washed up in the coves and on the beaches of Cornwall. However, the pieces that each beach received were mostly of a particular type of brick rather than an assortment. There had even been scientific studies done, he remembered, showing how the size and weight of the item depended on how far it floated before it was washed ashore. Following that logic, Aglets Cove was obviously in the perfect place for something the size and weight of a body to wash up onto. How very nice.

Steven's thoughts were lost in childhood memories of scouring the beaches for Lego dragons when something the reporter on the TV mentioned something that brought him back to the here and now. The victim was local.

'We now know that the body was that of John Helger, a native Cornishman from an old Cornish family that had always lived in Aglets Cove. He had lived in a secluded cottage along the cliff path and was known to be a bit of loner.' Steven was sure he had never met him, despite Nan's cottage being close by and, according to the reporter, nobody could remember when they last saw him. 'No one had even noticed he was missing.' Nothing unusual about that in the city Steven thought, but how sad that this could happen in a close village like Aglets. It was this casual attitude to life that had made leaving the city an easy decision. He hoped that this was just a one off and city life wasn't spreading out like a plague to envelope the rest of the country and the communities within it.

As Steven drove to the *Recorder's* offices, memories of his 'episode' on the beach the day before kept niggling at him, but he refused to give them consideration. He pushed aside the memory and his panic at what had happened to him that morning and tried to concentrate on his journey. If he didn't think about it, he didn't have to deal with it, that was his philosophy in life, and up to now it had always served him well. It was probably something to do with the after effects of seeing a dead body anyway. Nothing to concern him, nothing like it was likely to happen ever again, although he couldn't dislodge the uncomfortable feeling that it had happened before, somewhere in his past. A truth buried in a nightmare.

With that thought, the memory of his 'episode' seeped its way back into his conscious. Once again, he felt the freezing cold sea and the wind lashing at his face. He could remember himself singing in tune with a woman who mournfully wailed beside him and without thinking; he began to hum along to the tune. His foot hit the brake pedal, a woman wailing a song. He was sure that bit was new, or maybe he had heard it and forgotten that bit, but he couldn't be sure, and his mind began to feel as numb as his legs had been as he stood in the freezing sea.

The annoying buzzing and too cheerful cartoon music of his mobile's ringtone pulled him shivering from his brooding thoughts.

*The Cursed Shore*

'Hey Steven,' John Bates, the editor from the *Recorder* exclaimed, 'are you far from the cove?' Steven took a deep breath, a sense of dread creeping over him.

'Not far,' he said.

'Excellent!' came the reply. 'We have another body, a second one on the beach, did you hear me? Another body! Some coincidence, huh? As it's in your neck of the woods can you spin round and go and cover it for us?'

Steven was horrified, not particularly for the poor lost soul but because he could still remember the taste of the last victim lingering at the back of his throat. He knew he was the ideal person to visit the scene of the crime but the thought of going back onto that beach under the same circumstances brought bile up into his throat.

'This time it's a kid, not a child, no, young lad. Hasn't been identified yet, a surfer they said.' Steven grimaced, turned the car round again, and headed back to the cove wishing all Aglets lost souls were only plastic dragons.

The gravel crunched noisily under the car's tyres as he pulled into the car park. He was surprised to see how many people were already here, people he had never seen before, milling about aimlessly, yet doing their best to look officious. There was an obvious air of excitement despite the unfortunate circumstances.

He noticed a few locals deep in conversation; no doubt pondering the unfortunate coincidence, a great place to start. He casually walked over and joined the group trying not to look too much like a journalist.

'So, all a bit strange isn't it? Two bodies in two days,' he said.

'Aye that it is,' one of the men answered.

'Did you know the first victim? I heard he was from this village,' he asked.

'Maybe,' was all the answer he got.

Then they fell quiet and looked at him expectantly. He coughed and looked at his watch for no reason whatsoever then up at the entrance to the beach. 'Oh well,' he said, 'I suppose I should go and see what they know.'

'Good idea,' the man replied. They waited until Steven was a few feet away before continuing their conversation, but all Steven could hear was the murmuring of their lowered voices. He wasn't sure if it was because he was still too new to the village or if they simply didn't trust reporters poking their noses into village affairs, either way it was obvious they were not going to talk to him.

He made his way up the wooden steps that led to the beach but did not step on the sand this time. It wasn't that he was afraid to he told himself, it was just unnecessary. Instead, he got the details he needed from the constable who was stationed at the entrance to the cove; it was the same one he had spoken to yesterday. They exchanged a few pleasantries as Steven tried to break the ice and he was relieved that the constable was gracious enough not to mention the whole fainting and crying out thing. Still, he could not wait to get away from the cove as he rushed through his obvious questions and received the standard replies. Soon he had enough information for his report and once more found himself breathing a sigh of relief as he got back into his car and headed home to write up it up. Not a good way to start his new life here, he thought, not a good thing to happen to his favourite beach. He felt a pang of guilt and reminded himself that it was not a good thing to happen to the two victims either. He wondered if city life had desensitised him.

Steven phoned the office and asked if he could write his report up at home and email it in later, saying that he didn't feel well. A fair excuse, he thought, having had to deal with a death two days in a row. Luckily, John was sympathetic and readily agreed, wishing him well, and looking forward to reading the report later.

Once through the door of the cottage he relaxed as the oppressive weight of the stress lift from him. He was being ridiculous he told himself and feeling the need to cleanse

*The Cursed Shore*

himself of his stupid behaviour he stripped off and headed to the bathroom.

The shower was lukewarm but refreshing all the same and Steven let it wash all the remaining stress from his body as his mind worked over the change to the story he would be writing up. Two bodies on the same stretch of beach, was it too soon to call it the work of a serial killer? Initial reports were saying the surfer had drowned despite the calm summer weather and the fact that he was an award-winning surfer and an excellent swimmer. The time of death was assumed to be as little as an hour before the body had been found; according to the constable it didn't even smell yet. Steven was happy to just take his word for it. Apparently, the police had found and questioned the surfer's girlfriend who confirmed that he had not been out long, and she hadn't been expecting him to come back for some time. He would never come back now, a short life suddenly snuffed out without reason. Nothing about it seemed natural.

'Was there bruising?' Steven had asked Constable Trevan.

'Not that I'm aware of,' he had said.

'Nothing round the wrists, like Helger?' Steven had asked.

'Not sure I know what you mean,' the constable had replied, and Steven didn't know if he was being deliberately evasive or honestly just didn't know.

The constable had gone on to say how they could find no link to the first death apart from the beach itself and the drowning. All angles and possibilities were being looked at but nothing conclusive could be found at the present time. Steven knew it was police jargon for go away and stop asking questions. Not that he resented it. They both had their jobs to do. The police were doing all they could to reassure the villagers, however. They had doubled patrols in the area, were making door-to-door enquiries, questioning the locals and tourists alike, but still they had no witnesses and nothing to change the conclusion of accidental deaths.

Something else was bothering Steven, more than the second death, more than the feeling he had at the cove. The name on the constable's uniform had said Trevan. Steven was sure that was the name he had called out during his 'episode'. Hadn't the man asked why he called out his name when he had helped him up? Alternatively, had he been so confused he didn't remember seeing the name plate before and had called him only after seeing it? Whatever the reason, he didn't want to spend any more time thinking about it. The whole sorry experience needed to be forgotten and gotten over. He had a report to write up.

After he had showered and changed, Steven tried once again to concentrate on typing up his version of the story, but it was hard to stay on track. He had an evening planned in the company of his favourite barmaid, Sandra. It was exactly what he needed to take his mind off everything else that had been happening. Sitting at his laptop, he let his mind drift to a happier place as he thought about her. She was not as beautiful as some, but prettier than most and although her fiery red hair matched her moods, she was always fun to be with. He had met up with her several times when he came down to visit Nan at weekends and hoped that now he was living here things could get a little more serious between them. In her company, he would be guaranteed to forget his work and be able to relax again.

Steven arrived at Sandra's cottage a little earlier than he was expected. He was anxious for something to take his mind off the piles of paperwork waiting for him on his desk, he had only been here a day yet somehow, he seemed to have acquired a backlog. He didn't want to think any more about it though, he had had enough of drowned bodies lying on the wet sand, silently demanding answers.

*The Cursed Shore*

Arriving early at Sandra's house wasn't a problem however, as when she answered the door, she was ready, ready for anything it would seem, standing there in a black lacy mini dress with an eternally plunging neckline.

'Hey, let's skip dinner tonight and just enjoy the dessert,' he suggested hopefully.

Sandra folded her arms, her expression turning into an exaggerated scowl,

'Not on your life, Steven Pearn, there is a new Italian place in Padstow you'll be taking me to first, then we can take a romantic stroll along the beach, and maybe have a peek at the cove where the murders happened. How exciting would that be!'

'It's cordoned off,' Steven replied quickly. 'It's a murder scene, Sandra, not a tourist attraction.'

Sandra wrapped her arms slowly round him and pulled herself close and whispered in his ear.

'But they will let you in won't they, Steven, dear? Seeing as you are a journalist who is covering the story? We could at least try.'

Steven's heart sank as he realised he wasn't going to get out of this one. 'Oh god, not the cove, anything but the cove,' he mumbled.

'What's that?' Sandra called over her shoulder as she reached for her jacket.

'Nothing, sweetheart, if that's what you want, why not?' he said smiling at her, and then muttered under his breath, 'Shit!' Why had he agreed to that? He was a slave to his hormones he thought as he chuckled to himself and followed her out of the door.

Dinner was pleasant enough, and as usual Sandra's light and witty conversation was working wonders on Steven's mood, and her long legs and ample cleavage did a similar job on his hormones. The waiter arrived with the bill and as Steven fumbled in his jacket for his wallet, Sandra was already heading for the door. Steven took a long deep breath. Guess there's no avoiding the beach tonight, he thought grimly.

There was no police cordon stopping them from entering the cove, Steven tried not to show his disappointment as he trudged after the joyful Sandra. It was a warm evening and the clear sky glittered with a million stars. There was a light breeze, which blew Sandra's long red hair from her face as she ran along the sand, shoes in her hand, squealing in delight like a child as the cold water splashed over her feet. I could almost fall in love with her tonight, Steven thought, as he caught up to her and grabbed her arm and pulling her close. As he kissed her, he wondered why he had been so reluctant to come here tonight, it was so perfect.

Sandra wrapped her arms around his neck and drew him closer, pressing her body seductively into his. His body reacted in the usual way and he slid his hand down her back, trying to find the zip that held all the goodies in. As he reached the target and began to tease the zipper slowly down, he experienced a tingling sensation creep up his spine coupled with an intuition that they were being watched.

He quickly turned around, expecting to see another courting couple or maybe tourists, but apart from themselves, the beach was empty. He looked up to the coastal path, which wound its way along the clifftops, but there was nobody there either, none he could see anyway.

Steven shuddered as the now familiar sensation of dread, and a slight panic, crept over him again. It was just like the day the first body had washed up on the shore, he began to feel detached from reality. He gripped on to Sandra's shoulders as a wave of dizziness took him. He fought to control the panic, frightened it would overwhelm him, that he would lose control of his sanity because of it, and desperate for Sandra not to notice. There was nothing to be frightened of he told himself as he fought to keep his

*The Cursed Shore*

breathing slow and steady, there was no one here but Sandra and himself, but the feeling wouldn't go.

'What's wrong, babe?' Sandra murmured in his ear, unaware of the turmoil going on inside of him.

'Nothing, love,' he said, trying to sound convincing. 'Isn't it time we headed home?'

'But I want to stay on the beach,' she said, pouting and looking up at him. 'I want to make love under the stars tonight, don't you?' she said.

Steven was sure that he did not.

'You morbid pervert!' he laughed, the panic then left him as quickly as it had arrived, even so, he still didn't fancy staying any longer than he had to. 'Sorry Sandra, if you want my body tonight, you'll have to take me home first. I prefer a soft warm bed to sand in my pants, and other places.'

Sandra looked disappointed and for a moment he thought he had blown it, but he was in luck, smiling she put her arm through his and said, 'Then let's head for home, and quick!'

As they left the cove, Steven could not resist one more glance back at the beach. This time his heart jumped as he saw the shape of someone, standing on the cliff path just above the old mooring ring. Someone had been watching them after all and was watching still as they made their way up the beach. He could not help but think it might have been the murderer looking for his next victim rather than a local, although it was probably only a tourist wanting a peek at the crime scene. Steven wondered if he should inform the police, just in case, but Sandra was leaning into him, breathing softly into his neck. Whoever it was he would worry about it tomorrow; tonight he would lose himself in Sandra's arms. Grinning, he reached for his car keys and together they ran, laughing, back to the car.

# CHAPTER 5

A strong wind was beginning to blow across the beach, whipping the fine sand up into little mini sandstorms that searched for nooks and crannies to hide itself in his pristine uniform. Andrew Trevan turned his back against it and looked down at the travesty lying on the beach in front of him, another body on the sand for the whole world to see. It was another pathetic failure; how could it have gone so spectacularly wrong again? Soon, too many people would be asking the wrong, or maybe the right questions and that would only make things worse.

As he stood brooding over the morning's offerings, Sergeant Wheeler the Scene of Crimes Officer joined him.

'Another day, another body,' Andrew commented to his colleague. 'It's all fun and games this summer, isn't it?' The other officer nodded and raised a wry eyebrow at Andrew's forced cheerfulness, so Andrew thought it best to shut up and get on with his job. He scanned the cliff path; a few interested people were starting to gather, but no one was crass enough to be taking photos and no one was brave enough to come down the steps for a closer look. He wished they would, he could do with the distraction. He clasped his hands firmly behind his back to appear confident as well as official, yet he was trembling inside. The fainting man from yesterday had been sniffing around, asking questions. Andrew was horrified to find out that not only was he was a journalist but one that now lived in the village, and even worse, he was dating Sandra. This could make things very awkward.

*The Cursed Shore*

He looked down at the pale face of the young man who looked back up at him with that blue grey milky gaze dead bodies always had. Why were they being washed up into the cove? He wondered why couldn't the sea just take them away and be done with it. Why did it always have to bring them back?

Another officer came over to join Andrew.

'I see your fainting friend from yesterday was here again,' he said as he gestured towards the car park. 'Is he a person of interest?'

'Not really,' Andrew replied, 'turns out he is more of a pain in the arse. A journalist, looking to make an interesting story out of a couple of accidental deaths, I wish he would bother someone else about it.'

'Don't worry, Andrew. I'm sure he'll spell your name right when he puts you in the papers.' Andrew realised he was frowning deeply. He forced the lines from his face and put on his brightest smile.

'He'd better,' he said.

The other officer gave Andrew a playful pat on the back.

'Come on Andrew. Give us a hand getting this young lad off the beach. Don't want the seagulls getting hold of him as well.'

As Andrew and the SOCOs prepared to take the body away, Andrew was careful to make sure the marks on the boy's wrists were completely covered. He then followed the small procession off the beach and into the onslaught of questions from the locals who had gathered to hear a good story and were disappointed when their questions were evaded with the usual rote of an official statement would be made shortly.

A clean-up crew passed Andrew on their way to double check everything was as it should be on the beach before it could be opened to the public again. He heard them curse their luck at the airborne sand which would make the job that much harder. Andrew was sure that nothing strange or unusual would be found but still the sight of them and the thought of them prodding and poking around made him very uncomfortable.

For Trevan the on-site job was all finished, and they were driving back to the station to fill in the mountain of paperwork the inconsiderate wretch had caused. Blaming the victim was the best defence he had against any feelings of guilt that might try to trip him up.

Tonight would be better, he told himself sternly. It had to be, because another body on the beach tomorrow was going to be disastrous.

# CHAPTER 6

Steven groaned in his sleep, writhing, sweat-soaked like a sick man. His sheets twisted around his body as if tying him to his nightmare. His body may have been in his bed, but his mind was somewhere in the past on a stormy beach, shivering violently and wondering how he and his compatriots were going to get out of this mess.

'Should've cut us in like we arranged, Parson,' the head of the Revenue men yelled. 'Wouldn't 'ave cost no more than a barrel or two. Now look where all that greed has got you.'

Jacob, somehow his name was now Jacob, scowled at the cowering preacher as Trevan, the leader of the crooked Revenue gang, continued his lecture. 'It's not like I want you to suffer n'all.' He said, 'but there is a price to be paid one way or the other and you have got to pay it, see? Otherwise every smuggler along the coast will think they can get the better of us, and we can't have that can we brothers?' His fellow officers shook their heads seriously and murmured their snarling agreement through gritted teeth.

'We can come to a new agreement,' Jacob yelled back. 'If you arrest us there will be no more brandy or income from Aglets Cove for ever more for the likes of you. Where's the profit in that?' The Revenue men laughed at him as Trevan answered.

'Arrest you? Now why would we do that? T'aint a judge for twenty miles that don't profit from your little trade, no way you would get a conviction. No, we have our own little punishment in mind, one that'll send a clear

*Ellen Hiller*

message to all those others that be thinking of cutting us out of our fair share.'

Trevan nodded to his comrades, and they came down the stone steps and onto the beach, their loaded pistols pointing at the shivering smugglers as they stood dripping seawater on the already soaked beach.

Jacob took a deep breath and closed his eyes, waiting for the bang of the gun and the flare of light that would signal the end of his life. However, instead of the pain of a musket ball, he experienced the chill of cold iron as a set of manacles were attached to his wrists. He looked down in surprise then stumbled as he was yanked along by a length of iron chain to the cliff side of the cove. The other smugglers soon joined him as they were all chained together to a large iron ring that had long ago been set into the stone at the side of the cliff face. The ring was normally used to moor the village's small rowing boats, but these had since been cut free by the Revenue men and were now making their own way out into the rough sea. Jacob pictured himself in one of them, safely washed away with the tide, and wished that it were true.

Realising what the Revenue intended for them, Jacob panicked and pulled back on the chain with all his strength until one of the Revenue gang, John Helger, whacked the back of his legs with a baton. His legs buckled under the blow, and he was shoved forwards far enough for Trevan to attach the chain to the mooring ring where he joined the rest of his confused and frightened kinfolk.

Jacob and the others pulled and tugged against the thick iron chain that bound him to the rock, but nothing gave, not even a fraction. They pleaded and cried for mercy, but the Revenue men just sniggered and shook their heads.

The tide had turned and soon the sea would be making its way back into the cove. Still time for them to release us, Jacob thought with a glimmer of hope, but the Revenue men showed no sign of changing their minds.

*The Cursed Shore*

It wasn't long before the water was lapping round Jacob's ankles, weak and shallow for now, but not for long. Not wanting to get their feet wet, Trevan's Revenue gang walked further up the beach, away from the stricken smugglers, and as they retreated so did all hope of mercy.

Jacob knew the sea would take his life, knew that he could not fight it and that knowledge fuelled his panic with rage. He lashed out, he roared, he wailed at the injustice of it all, until one of his fellow captives, old Davy Denman, shoved him violently in the back.

'Aint no use complaining is there?' Denman spat. 'We are going to die anyways, don't let them have the satisfaction of them knowing you is scared.' Jacob snarled back like an animal at the man, lost in his own personal panic as the water calmly yet relentlessly rose, now reaching up to chill his knees, he didn't care if the Revenue men knew it or not, he was terrified.

The tide always rolled fast into the cove and as the water deepened, small waves formed, crashing into their trembling legs, and washing away the sand beneath their feet causing them to stumble and stagger and pull against their chains to remain upright.

Jacob never thought it would end like this. He knew smuggling was a risk, but one that had to be taken if they were to survive the harsh winters that blasted the village. The money he earned from it stocked the larders and filled the shed with wood for the fire. It wasn't done for luxury it was a necessity. If he had been caught, he could accept being shot or even hanged for his crimes, but this was cruel and inhumane and none of them deserved it. Being restrained like an animal among his kinfolk and left on the shoreline to drown slowly at the leisure of the cruel cold sea, that had never been in his reckoning.

A wave hit him hard and sea spray splashed up into his face mingling with the rain that poured from the dark heavens above until he was sure that he was already drowning with the seawater yet to reach his waist.

*Ellen Hiller*

From somewhere behind him a woman's voice started chanting, it was Sarah Scadden, the village wise woman, healer, midwife, attendant to the deceased, and witch. The voice was shaky and cried through chattering teeth but there was no mistaking the menace behind the words. Parson Willoughby growled at her. 'Someone shut that damned witch up,' He shouted. 'Godforsaken bitch will damn us all to Hell.'

No one shut her up. The smugglers of Aglets Cove may have sung hymns at Parson Willoughby's church on a Sunday morning, but if they wanted something spiritual done, it was Sarah Scadden they went to. It was her magic they trusted not his. Now their hearts thudded to the beat of her song, they could feel the vengeance in her words and welcomed it. The ancient chant tugged at their souls and drew on their fear, and even though they were words that they had never heard voiced before, they knew the meaning.

The revenue men could also guess the meaning, Trevan especially. Nervously he looked around him and then up into the dark sky wondering if he was about to be struck by a thunderbolt. He growled a warning at his fellow customs officers, but they looked at him with bewildered expressions.

As Sarah's voice climbed higher, it seemed to hush the splash of the waves and the roar of the sea and the prisoners stopped struggling and poured their own thoughts and hatred and despair into the strange sounds she made, their screams and wails falling in with the erratic tune. With the added voices, the words gained power. Then it was as if the wind itself howled the same tune as the breaking waves beat the rhythm of a song from an older time.

The Revenue men staggered backwards as the power and the intent of the song reached out to them. They looked at each other seeking reassurance and finding only frightened faces that matched their own, ran back up the beach and up the worn granite steps that led up to the cliff path without looking back. In a panic to get past his own men, Jory Trevan shoved his friend and comrade Thomas Dyer near off the steps and onto the rocks below. Dyer hissed an insult and shoved Trevan back along the rocky path, all this had been his idea and now he wondered, and not for the first time, why he always followed Trevan's command without question. They could have chosen to turn back and free the prisoners, they could have said they only meant to frighten them, to teach them a lesson but they could not stop now, they were driven on by their fear.

They kept running and left the Aglets Cove villagers behind to drown. They ran as fast as they could, through the sleepy lanes and dirt roads not stopping until they were back to the supposed safety of their homes where they secured bolts and latches against the unseen. They thought they would be safe there; they thought that they could outrun a witch's death curse.

They were wrong.

Now the smugglers were alone on the beach with no hope of the Revenue men changing their minds. Jacob stared menacingly at Parson Willoughby who by now was half floating beside him, head lolled back and eyes staring sightlessly to the heavens he claimed to represent. It was all his fault. Most of the village folk had agreed to cut the revenue men in on the smuggling to ensure they turned a blind eye when needed. However, the greedy parson wanted none of it and used his authority and fear of the church to bring the rest of them to his side.

Jacob tried to barge the drowned parson away from himself, not wanting it to be the last thing he saw, then closed his eyes in horror as the body floated straight back at him filling his vision with its huge vacant eyes and gaping mouth. He pushed it again, this time to the side of him and turned his back so he could no longer see the grotesque expression, knowing his own face would shortly be its mirror.

*Ellen Hiller*

The sea had reached his neck at last, and he was already on the edge of consciousness due to its cold embrace, one that he hoped he would succumb to that before drowning, but luck proved as elusive as hope had been. A surging wave caught him off guard and the seawater surged into his mouth and throat causing the muscles within to spasm closed, cutting off his airways as it tried to protect his lungs. Jacob found he could not have breathed in the water even if he wanted to, although to do so would at least have quickened his death and ended his ordeal. His lungs ached for another precious gasp of air and as his mouth broke free of the water, he tried to take another quick breath, forcing the air down, passed the clenched muscles of his throat, an unholy groaning sound escaping as he did so. Too soon, the next wave came, and his face was underwater again. He struggled to hold on to that precious breath for what he was sure was hours but inevitably, little by little it trickled its way out of his mouth, one bubble at a time.

The wave started to retreat once more, and Jacob tried to stand on tiptoe, stretching himself as high as he could, hoping beyond hope to catch another breath, but the chance never came. Another wave rolled in before the last had fully left and this time it covered his head completely. He knew he would never surface again. The panic that had been building to a crescendo rushed away from him until there was nothing left to fight the surge of the water following its new pathway to his lungs.

The fight was over, his body relaxed involuntarily as the darkness and the cold took him and life became an irrelevant memory, the only thoughts lingering in his head were of the curse and the names of those who had killed him.

Steven awoke from the nightmare, choking and gasping for breath. For a while he could do nothing but sit there heaving in air, one forced breath at a time. He clutched the

*The Cursed Shore*

side of the mattress waiting for the world to stop spinning, waiting for the memory of the sea to diminish as he stared at the mundane pink flowery wallpaper, hoping for reality to take hold.

At last, when the world emerged as the familiar one, the one without the drowning, without the fear, without the hatred and the strange singing, Steven pulled the duvet back around himself needing its warm comfort and security.

He looked out of the window, the sun was slowly rising over the horizon promising a lovely day, but a cold chill left him shuddering, a primal survival instinct telling him to stay here where it was safe and dry and to stay away from the danger of the cove.

Steven mentally slapped himself to get rid of the last strands of the nightmare and forced himself to get out of bed. He pulled the duvet off and wrapped it around himself as he waddled downstairs to the kitchen. It was going to be a warm summer's morning, so he didn't need the heat, but he refused to let it go. He prepared his usual coffee and croissant, with the duvet still hanging around him like a cape, settled himself on the sofa, and opened his laptop.

Checking in on his social media accounts was enough to push the nightmare away and soon Steven was back to his old self. Time, he thought to get some work done. He still had a story to type up, and then he could get started on clearing out and decorating the cottage. It was going to be sad getting rid of Nan's things but that flowery wallpaper in the bedroom had to be the first thing to go.

# CHAPTER 7

Steven rubbed his forehead trying to erase the dull headache that was embedded there. His eyes felt tired and gritty from hours of searching the internet, looking for background information on the two victims. He still hoped to find a link between the murders. Maybe he would find something the police had missed. It was fruitless though. There was plenty to be found on the poor surfer, but the old guy, unlike the youth of today, had lived a life far away from the internet. Digitally he did not exist.

Normally Steven would have been content to report whatever the police had officially released and to wait patiently until that time. This time, however, because it had been dropped quite literally on his doorstep, he felt more involved. He was the one to find the first body, so he had a personal interest in the story, and he was not prepared to wait for an official report and be told half-truths by the local police constable.

Never liking or feeling at home with city life, Steven had been ecstatic to come back to live in Cornwall, not only because of the convenience of inheriting Nan's cottage but for the relaxed living in a beautiful serene setting. Having bodies dumped on the beach was not part of that plan and he wanted rid of the story and a return to normality as soon as possible.

He had spent the previous afternoon questioning half the village and so far, all he had discovered was that both men had old Cornish names, and both had an ancestry in this area, which seemed to go back for generations. The most curious fact to him, though not to the police it would

*The Cursed Shore*

seem, was the fact that for both men it was their first time visiting the beach. Simon Dyer's girlfriend had confirmed that it was his first time surfing the cove and even old John Helger, despite living on the edge of the cliff path, had apparently never stepped foot on the sand. He had often told neighbours that he had an aversion to beaches and never intended to get any closer than the cliffs. Steven found himself sympathising with this immensely, which gave him reason to pause and wonder, maybe he was not the only person to have experienced something strange there.

Opening his laptop again, he typed in a new search query, 'History of Aglets Cove, Cornwall'.

Several hours later, he slammed the lid of the laptop down, hoping it would shut him off from the bizarre thoughts spinning in his head. There would be no chance of that however, and he slumped back into the chair and tried to make logical sense of what he had read.

If local legend was to be believed, a group of local smugglers had been murdered on the beach by Revenue officers in 1796 and according to local myth their souls had haunted the cove ever since. One of the smuggler's names was Jacob Pearn. Steven tried to remember the details of his dream, wasn't he called Jacob? It was hard to recall, had this dream Jacob been a real person? An ancestor of his maybe? It was all so very bizarre. The story didn't end with the murders however, there was apparently a witch's death curse of revenge put on the men that murdered the smugglers. Apparently, that curse had kept those related to the Revenue men from visiting the cove for generations. Steven shifted uneasily on his seat; his half-forgotten nightmare had grown legs and was beginning to run.

Unfortunately, the internet could only provide Steven with a brief outline of the story, but it was enough to pique his interest. After the initial horror, a thrill of excitement set his pulse racing, what a story this could be. He knew

*Ellen Hiller*

there must be a connection here; the nightmares were too real to just be a fantasy.

Steven needed to find out more about Jacob Pearn and if or how they could be related. His first step would be the local parish records, and then maybe interviewing a few of the older folk of the village; there had been some he had not wanted to bother before, that was a mistake. The Cornish loved their fireside tales of wreckers and smugglers and no doubt, a story such as this would have been passed down over the years by the older village folk that lived hereabouts.

Steven wasn't sure how any of this could be connected to the present day, maybe a local murderer knew about the cove's history and thought it would make Aglets a good place to dump their victims' bodies. Whatever the reason he now knew however, of a more interesting, more entertaining, twist to the story than the murders alone. The witches curse on the families of the Revenue men. He hoped that if the big papers sniffed out a story, they would not think to check the historical records as he had done. If they didn't, the story would be his alone.

Steven began to imagine his story on the front pages of the national papers, sat back in his chair, and smiled. Maybe he could get a book deal from this, maybe even a movie. Then realising he could spend the rest of the daydreaming about the consequences of an investigation he had barely even started yet, opened the laptop again to search for the parish records online, hoping for exact dates for the deaths of the smuggling villagers. A large group dying on the same day would also give him more names to work with as he further researched the story. Unfortunately, although to him, unsurprisingly, the records for Aglets Cove had yet to be digitalised. He would have to check them for himself at the local county office. He decided he could fit this in after interviewing the locals; after all, they might throw up some more names and information for him to check on. He shrugged the duvet

*The Cursed Shore*

from his shoulders and ran upstairs to get dressed. He loved to get his teeth into a piece of juicy research; today was going to be fun.

First things first, Steven phoned the *Recorder* office and told John he had come down with a bug. As expected, John said for him to take a few days off. Steven guessed he would only need a couple.

Fumbling through the old record books at the local county office and inhaling the musky smell that spoke more of the ages past than the dates on the pages, he found himself absorbed in the history of the cove and with it his family. Steven had never been into genealogy, but he found it exciting as through the records, he was able to trace his father's family name back through the years and cross-indexed it with the local history he had learned of earlier. It felt like travelling back in time. He shuddered as a whisper of his nightmare flittered across his mind as he mentally pushed it aside.

He had known that his family was firmly rooted in the Cornish soil, sand, and sea, although he, himself, had grown up in Bristol. Now reading his family's history, he was amazed to find out just how far back into the history of Aglets Cove the Pearn family name went.

His search eventually took him back to 1796 when his ancestor was indeed one of a group of villagers to die on the same day with drowning as a cause of death. It had been what he was looking for but still it shocked him to see it. In a strange way he had wanted it to be untrue, just his wild imagination building a story out of a nightmare, but it wasn't so. He quickly jotted the names down then left for the local library to look at the microfiche of local papers and journals that went back for centuries.

He was on a roll and found it hard to contain his excitement as he struggled not to speed along the narrow lanes that took him to the library. Once there, he wasted no time in setting up for the long haul that was in front of

*Ellen Hiller*

him. He knew from experience that he was going to have to read a lot of rubbish before he found what he had come for. However, he was a journalist; he knew it would be worth it.

His eyes were sore from staring at so much irrelevant information, his back ached, and he wished the seats here were cushioned. Eventually he found it, the holy grail, nineteen local men and women all thought to be involved in the smuggling of brandy, tobacco and tea all found dead on the beach, drowned.

Although nothing had been proved, it was hinted heavily that the revenue men had been cut out of a deal and took their revenge on the members of the gang as they unloaded a boat in Aglets Cove one night. It was a harsh and effective lesson to others who might have had similar thoughts.

As well as his own the other two names he was expecting were there in the report, Helger and Dyer, they were both Revenue officers thought to be involved in the killings. Both names were not common names, even in Cornwall but here was a confirmation of the link he had been looking for, a possibly murderous Helger, and a dead Helger, the first body to be found on the beach. A Revenue man named Dyer and now a dead surfer with the same name. Steven doubted it got any stranger than this, and then he noticed another name, a name that made his breath catch in his throat.

It was obvious it would be there but seeing it in black and white in front of him added a dimension of reality he wasn't sure he was ready for. Trevan. Just as in his dreams, one of the murderous Revenue men was called Trevan. His own ancestor a renowned smuggler from this very area had been killed by him and Steven had no doubt that this Trevan was related to the Constable Trevan he had met on the beach.

A familiar feeling of iced water in his veins spread from his heart outwards as panic threatened to overwhelm

*The Cursed Shore*

him for a moment, only this time the feeling was tinged with an unreasonable amount of anger. As he thought more about the unlikely connection, he rose sharply from his seat as he mentally fought being pulled away from the safety of reality and into the world of his nightmare once again. This was 2019, and he wasn't living in some sort of movie, it was real life. This sort of thing simply did not happen he told himself firmly.

Taking deep breaths to try to slow his mind and steady his nerves he managed to bring himself back to the here and now. There had to be a rational explanation for what seemed impossible, he just hadn't made all the connections yet.

Steven slumped back down into the chair pushing the microfiche reader away from himself as he did so. He wished he could just as easily push away the story it told.

The increasingly familiar sense of being watched crept over him with its tingling fingers running up his spine, and he turned to see old Miss Doryty standing by the desk eyeing him curiously whilst sweeping a broom around. Steven smiled and nodded to her; he hadn't realised she worked as the cleaner here.

'You know you've been here hours looking over them old records?' Old Miss Doryty said. 'It was time for me to lock up two hours past, but I didn't like to disturb you.' Steven muttered his thanks, slightly embarrassed about being caught looking at the old stories, though he didn't know why. He looked out of the window and was shocked to see that the bright sunny day had turned into evening as he had worked. How did he lose so much time without realising it?

The woman moved closer eyeing the ancient newspaper on the microfiche, a strange smile on her face.

'Not the first old name to end up dead on the beach you know,' she looked Steven in the eyes with a cold steely stare that made him uncomfortable.

*Ellen Hiller*

'I, err umm, I'm sorry, what do you mean?' he said, stumbling over his words and switching it off like a 14-year-old caught looking at online porn. Old Doryty leaned in close to his ear.

'You widen your search; you'll find more than one death on that beach, all with old names, all with revenue men's names,' she said and withdrew back to where she had stood by the desk. 'When you need more help, come see old Doryty,' she said as she smiled benevolently at him.

Forgetting the late hour, Steven turned the microfiche reader on again and began looking for all the names of all the Revenue men rumoured to be involved in the incident. He glanced up to ask the old woman what more she knew and was surprised to see that she had gone, the lights were off, and he was alone. He wondered if he was locked in, but the idea didn't bother him, he had a lot of research to do and he likely wouldn't be ready to leave till morning.

Seven a.m. saw him finished and packed up again just as the door was unlocked and the caretaker walked in, shocked to find him standing there. Steven did not stop to explain; all he could think of were the words dancing around his head. One paragraph in particular had grabbed his attention, along with a faded picture of a jolly looking man in a newspaper clipping.

'... he waded out into the water to save the stricken sailor only to lose his footing and himself plunge into the icy sea never to be seen again despite the shallowness of depth. They said he had been swept out to sea by a freak wave but there are some folk that tell a different story. Others that were on the beach that day say they saw ghostly hands pulling the man under. Some say it was the ghosts of the Aglets Cove smugglers....'

His earlier fantasy now seemed achievable as the words 'book deal' etched themselves firmly in his mind, this really was big with the potential to be epic, and he was right here in the middle of it, with a family connection to the whole story. The potential for fame conveniently overriding the unnatural aspects of the case so he didn't have to think too hard about it.

After a quick nap and a bite to eat, he would look in on old Miss Doryty. Clearly, she knew more about this local legend, perhaps even first-hand stories passed down through the generations. Any anecdotes he could get from her would be priceless.

Grinning like a maniac with a purpose he drove back home. He could not believe his luck in stumbling on the connections before anyone else. This was everything he had been waiting for and so much more, but first he needed to catch up on some sleep. His head was muzzy, and he was sure his whole body had doubled in weight, what he needed was a full night's sleep without nightmares, but for now a nap until lunchtime would suffice.

Steven plumped up the pillows and pulled the duvet back. The bed looked cosy and inviting and he longed to throw himself into it, to snuggle up and drift off into oblivion. That is how it used to be, how it should be. Beds are a place of comfort and security, the place to relax and leave your cares and worries of the day behind you.

He yawned and sat down on the edge. Maybe this time he would not die, maybe this time his dreams would take him away from the cold and unforgiving sea.

He was so tired, his head spun with every slight movement, he had to lie down, and there was no fighting it. He closed his eyes and tried to clear his mind. Immediately Steven felt himself drifting off and jerked himself awake again. He turned over and tried again and once more.

However, the moment he experienced that lightheaded drifting of thought that came before oblivion he woke himself up once more, it was an involuntary thing, as if his body was protecting him from the horrors that awaited his unconscious mind. It kept happening repeatedly until eventually he toyed with the idea of getting up again. Then he opened his eyes, and he was waist deep in freezing seawater, chained to an iron mooring ring, screaming in terror.

The part of him that was still Steven Pearn knew it to be a dream, but he was no less trapped by it. He still experienced the terror, the cold, and the despair. He still knew the hatred and heard the witches chant and as the water pushed his way down his throat, he wished with all his heart and soul, and anger, for Trevan to suffer the same fate.

Then he drowned.

Steven awoke at home in bed, at first relieved that it was over but then panic struck as he tried to breathe, but his lungs would not open. He tried harder producing an unholy groaning sound as a small amount of precious air trickled through. It wasn't enough. He threw himself out of the bed trying to distance himself from the nightmare, but he still couldn't breathe. He collapsed down on to all fours and retched, trying to clear his lungs of whatever was blocking the air. A small amount of drool dribbled down his chin, and he tried again to force the air in, but it seemed the harder he tried the more resistance was there. He was dizzy now, he knew he would pass out soon, and then what? Would he die? Through his frantic thoughts, he saw the newspaper headlines:

*Man drowns in bed.*

His body convulsed involuntary. Huge wracking heaves that bent him in two so violently he thought he was in the midst of his death throes. Then he vomited water, lots of water. It didn't smell or taste of bile, it smelt and tasted of the sea and as his lungs pushed the last of the water out, Steven breathed in a mercifully long gasp of air.

This time there was nothing to stop it filling his lungs, and he sat back and enjoyed the feeling of breathing each breath repeatedly, how he had taken the act for granted before he never knew. Breathing was beautiful and wholesome, and he was alive and able to do it.

When at last, the breathing quietened and normality crept back into his world, Steven tried to analyse what had just happened. Had he sleepwalked into the ocean? Impossible, his clothes were dry. Maybe he had vomited in his sleep and choked on it? That's what it felt like, but then why did it taste of seawater?

There was nothing rational here, nothing.

When he felt strong enough, and the fear had left him Steven cleaned up the mess and refused to think any more about it. It was something else to push to the back of his mind to deal with 'later'. It was getting crowded back there, he thought.

# CHAPTER 8

Andrew Trevan walked across Peter Enys's potato field towards the edge where it met the cliff path, the place where the bonfires were always lit. He carefully steered around the full-grown potato plants with his wheelbarrow as he went, Peter would not be happy if any of his precious crop were damaged. The barrow was full of wood and kindling for tonight's ritual. The wood collecting and fire preparation was always Andrew's job; he liked to be the one to set everything up. Everything had to be done just so, and he knew he was the only one of them that had the eye for the finer details, so it had to be him. He was also aware that the others lacked the ability to prepare the site in accordance with the rules in the way he could, but he knew that it wasn't kind to mention it, so he didn't. He simply assured them it was his job and they let him get on with it.

Once at the ritual site, Andrew used a shovel to clear away the ash from yesterday's fire, piling it against the low slate wall at the edge of the field. There it joined ash piles both new and ancient to mingle and rot, seeping into the ground or blown out to sea by the wind. Wherever it went, there was always lots of it but never too much as to be a problem. Must be magic, he thought to himself as he worked, then chuckled at his own joke as he had done so many times before.

Once the ash was cleared, he used the shovel blade to carve a pentagram deep into the black burnt dirt. The markings from the previous ritual were always visible and as usual, he used these to guide him, making sure the new

*The Cursed Shore*

lines were sharp and clear. As he worked, he spoke the words of the spell invoking the elements of water, fire, earth, and air to bind his words. This done he piled on the fresh wood and kindling on top making sure there were enough gaps to ensure good airflow to the fire.

After he double-checked that the fire was good to go, Andrew set to work on the perimeter, re-carving the ancient symbols with his knife whilst speaking their names and meanings and letting the power flow from his body through the knife and into each marking.

As he worked Andrew's mind wandered back to the day Marjory had brought him here to teach him how to carve the sigils so many years ago. Her firm hand had steadied his trembling one and as they worked the markings together she whispered the words in his ear that he then spoke aloud and as he did so, he felt the power flow through her and into him and then into the soil and the sigils he had carved.

He smiled at the memory then took another clean knife from his jacket pocket and sliced it through his already scarred hand. The blood flowed freely, and he carefully dribbled a small amount on each of the six symbols. Marjory never flinched when she drew the blade across her palm that day but despite his bravado, he winced and had to force himself not to inspect the depth of the wound as his blood flowed freely into the thirsty soil.

'Blood for blood,' she had told him. 'When you ask for a thing, you give something precious in return, balance, there must always be a balance.'

Now he understood more than he had that first day and now when he performed the ritual, his hand was as steady as hers had been, and the words flowed unbidden from his lips as easy as the blood flowed from his wounded hand.

When he was finished, he sat on the stone wall and gazed out to sea and relaxed as he bandaged his bloody hand and cleaned his knives. This was the best part of the whole ritual for him, sitting in solitude with the magic around him and feeling its connection to the sea in front of him. The modern world and all its disbeliefs could not touch him here. This was his domain, and he controlled it.

# CHAPTER 9

After his disastrous nap, Steven sat wrapped in his duvet in front of the TV. He wasn't really watching though, he just let the images flitter unconsciously through his numb mind until without asking permission his body fell into a deep sleep that unwittingly lasted for the rest of the day and the whole of the night too. His body was claiming the rest it needed whilst leaving his mind in the constant loop of the nightmare. At times, he would feel consciousness returning as he struggled to open his eyes, only to be dragged back down into the watery depths.

Eventually, the sun rose once more, and its brightness rescued Steven from further trauma. He sat up sharply, refusing to let sleep claim him again. He was still exhausted despite the hours he had slept, and so he wrapped the duvet tight around himself until it felt like a hug as he tried to make sense of the memory of his dreams.

The dark images still flitted across his mind like wisps of mist that he tried to grab and study before they dissipated, but he was never quite able to grasp them. He wept like a child and wished this would go away and happen to someone else for a change. He wished he wasn't alone in the word and that he could amble into the kitchen to share the story of his nightmares over breakfast with his family. Where his mother would make him tea and cook breakfast and his dad would find a way of turning the nightmares into a joke that they would all laugh at, and then forget about, as they ate their morning meal together.

*Ellen Hiller*

The fact that those days were long gone now, hurt as much as the nightmare itself.

As the morning sun chased the nightmares away once more, Andrew reminded himself he was an adult, his parents were not here, and he had to deal with it himself. He needed to get up right now and pull himself together, and so, reluctantly, he did. Making his way zombie-like into the kitchen he bounced off walls and doorframes till he dropped the duvet and forced himself to stop walking like a Neanderthal and to stand upright. He needed coffee and food before he was going to feel even remotely human though.

As he sat with his head bowed over his coffee mug, he prayed to whatever god might be listening that there wouldn't be another body on the beach today. His brain needed a break if he was ever going to make any sense of what he had discovered last night.

Relief washed over Steven when he remembered that Sandra was coming around today. Time spent with her was always a good distraction. It was just what he needed to bring him back to reality. He busied himself getting ready for the day, forcibly pushing all thoughts of his nightmares from his mind, refusing to give it any more time than had been stolen from him already. He also poured himself several more mugs of coffee in a bid to shake the half-asleep grogginess that had bugged him these last few days. Eventually he was bright and sprightly and on a wonderful caffeine high. The best way to start the day.

Sandra arrived early, bringing all the warmth of the summer's day in with her. She hugged Steven warmly and asked how he was. Steven froze, unable to wash everything away with a lie. Don't spoil the moment he told himself, you need today to be carefree and fun.

'Come on, out with it, what's wrong?' she asked, she looked worried and genuinely concerned, and that was all it took for the floodgates to open and everything flowed

*The Cursed Shore*

from him nonstop until Sandra was saturated with his grief and anxiety. When he had finished, he forced himself to meet her gaze and nervously asked her what she thought. She seemed to be unphased by his bizarre story and asked him in a calm practical voice.

'Are you sure you're remembering things in the correct order? Perhaps the nightmares begun after the research in the library and it's just your overactive imagination at work.'

It wasn't the reaction he expected, and Steven tried not to glare at her, after all she was only trying to make sense of the senseless, as he had been trying to do himself for the last few days. After he calmly assured her that this was not the case, she went on with her analysis. 'Well something is clearly wrong, maybe it's something to do with the move down here. It is a big upheaval in your life, especially having to clear out your nan's cottage. Have you registered with the local doctor yet? Maybe you should consider therapy, dear. Talking to someone about the nightmares might help.'

Sandra had sat patiently whilst he mournfully told her of his nightmares and inability to sleep. It had felt good to share his experiences with her initially but now he just felt stupid. He had, in fact, considered therapy and further considered that he did not want to be certified as insane. There was no way he was going to a doctor about this.

'A bit too soon for therapy, isn't it? Besides, I don't think it would be any different from talking to you about it, Sandra. Who knows, maybe now I have told you everything, the nightmares might stop.' He didn't believe it for a second, but he did not want to discuss the matter anymore. How could a grown man tell a doctor he was having trouble with a reoccurring nightmare?

Nightmares, however, was not an adequate word to describe the terror that besieged his sleeping mind when he slept, but he doubted a more accurate word existed. Every night he died a slow awful death. It wasn't a dream to him;

*Ellen Hiller*

it was a physical thing. It was torture. He experienced the cold and the panic; and winced at the pain of the manacles biting further into wrists as he pulled against the chain. He heard the wailing of the wind and the crashing of the waves, as they got closer and closer. Then when his dream-self drowned, he awoke choking as if he had inhaled the seawater as he slept. That nightly experience carried its panic into his waking hours threatening to strip away his sanity. If it kept on, he feared, there would be no more Steven Pearn, but instead the shell of someone called Jacob, a jabbering wreck, rocking back and forth and moaning to himself about curses in the corner of an asylum.

Unfortunately, Sandra was not going to let it go, sitting next to him on the sofa, pulling him close.

'The doctor could help in other ways,' she said softly. 'They say the drugs do actually work, you know.'

Steven pulled himself away from her grip and sat up to face her.

'I'm not psychotic, Sandra! Something real is happening to me!' he snapped. However, as soon as the words left his mouth, he realised how psychotic he sounded. No doubt every lunatic in the asylum thought that they were the sane one, it was everyone else that was losing their mind.

'But maybe…' Sandra didn't continue the sentence and Steven knew she must be weary of trying to help him when he refused to listen or be helped.

A memory scratched at the back of his mind asking to be let in. It was old Miss Doryty, what did she say now? Something about if ever he needed help. It wasn't the words though; it was the implication. It had sounded weird at the time, the way she had said it, but here and now, he could not help but wonder if she had known what he was experiencing. She knew about the connection between the Revenue men and the recent deaths, and he was sure she had witnessed his panic attack on the beach, maybe she

*The Cursed Shore*

had been affected too. Maybe, thought Steven, a glimmer of hope rising amid all the gloom, maybe she would understand, help even.

'I have to go,' he declared as he all but jumped out of his seat.

'Go where?' Sandra asked. Her puzzled and overly concerned look revealing that, to her, his madness was escalating.

'To see Miss Doryty,' he called back as he flung the door open. 'Are you coming?'

'No, I am not!' Sandra stated as she screwed her face up in disgust. 'I didn't even know you knew her, horrible old woman she is.'

Steven stood, hesitating, at the open door, he wasn't expecting that.

'Why so much hate? She's just a little old lady, and I bet she has loads of local knowledge.'

'You're going to her for what knowledge exactly? How to stop your nightmares?'

'Yes, and no.' Steven wasn't sure how to explain. 'She could help with my research but…' he stopped. It was frustrating trying to explain it to her. Now he wished she hadn't visited today and that he hadn't told her about the nightmares. She was intruding on his personal thoughts and actions, not trying to help. He realised that he didn't want her to be involved in this part of his life, her knowledge of his nightmares now made him feel vulnerable and over exposed. Time for a new tactic.

'You know what, Sandra? You're right. Forget all this rubbish I've just had a bad night and haven't been able to shake it off yet. Let's do something fun instead, best kind of therapy.' He shut the door and with a false smile plastered on his face walked into her open arms. Later he would make an excuse to get rid of her.

Then he would visit Doryty.

# CHAPTER 10

Old Miss Doryty's cottage was a short drive from his own, easily within walking distance but that wasn't something Steven was used to doing. The cottage was typical of the area, it was small and squat with a thatched roof and small windows, and a garden full of English country flowers and climbing roses. Built using local granite stone it looked like it had stood firm throughout the centuries without need of change or modernisation.

As Steven walked up the path and knocked gently on the old wooden door, he noticed it was very old and rotten in places with the paint peeling off showing glimpses of previous shades of green paint. He guessed the door had lasted as long as the cottage itself, no doubt protected by its many layers of green.

A smiling Doryty welcomed him in as if she had been expecting him at that exact time, which helped to alleviate some of his awkwardness. There was a little patter of much smaller footsteps and an angry looking calico cat joined them. Steven tried not to grimace, it wasn't that he was afraid of cats or allergic to them, he just didn't like them, especially the way they always seemed to be judging him. From the look on this one's face he was sure he didn't come up to its very high feline standards. Doryty beckoned him in and he had to duck under the old wooden doorframe to enter.

Once through the door, the quaintness came to an abrupt halt. The small room he stepped into looked more like an ancient apothecary than the sitting room of an elderly lady. Dusty shelves lined all four walls, most of

*The Cursed Shore*

them laden with bottles and jars with faded handwritten labels. There were strange statues and exotic-looking bowls and enough candles to keep the whole village lit in the event of a blackout. From the ceiling there hung bunches of dried flowers and herbs, so dried that they had shrivelled and shed leaves and brown petals onto the worn floorboards below. Steven winced at the dusty chaos and couldn't resist pushing some of the crumbled herbs on the floor into a neat pile with his foot.

In the middle of the room facing the window were two comfortable looking chairs with a small table between. Steven hovered next to one waiting for an invitation to sit.

'Don't you be standing there waiting for an invitation, young man, make yourself comfortable,' said Doryty.

Steven sat down in one of the overstuffed chairs; it was as comfortable as it looked, and he started to relax. He decided to break the ice with the usual small talk about the weather and the tourists. Meanwhile Doryty pottered around him gathering up random items from the shelves and throwing them into a large cardboard box.

'My sister's things,' she explained, throwing in something that looked like a shrunken goat's head, with obvious distaste. 'Don't like doing it but it's past time it was all sorted. But then you understand that, don't you, dear, what with your nan and all?'

Steven agreed and Doryty put the box down, sat in the other chair, and gave him a motherly look.

'Now you tell me what's bothering you, all of it, and then we can have some tea and cake while we decide what's to be done about it.'

Steven's shoulders slumped as the last of the tension left his body. There was something about Doryty that exuded patience and understanding. Sitting in the comfortable chair while its ample stuffing embraced him, he realised that he felt more at home here than he did back in Nan's cottage.

*Ellen Hiller*

There was only a moment to enjoy the comfort however, because at that moment the cat decided to join him and jumped, without invitation, onto his lap. It immediately beginning to knead him into a more comfortable shape and Steven winced at the sharp pain of claws penetrating through his thin cotton trousers. Not wanting to upset Doryty, Steven ignored the pain as best he could and patted the cat gently on the head whilst at the same time trying to manoeuvre it into a position that did not threaten either his clothing or his skin.

Whilst micromanaging the cat, Steven told Doryty his story, the whole thing, more than he had revealed to Sandra. He was surprised how comfortable he was telling the old lady, including how the experience affected him emotionally as well as physically. Steven concluded the story with something he had tried not to think about but that wouldn't go away. '... and all the time I'm dreaming it I have this awful hatred of Constable Trevan. Not the old Revenue man called Trevan, but the police officer that lives here and now, in this village. I can't even bring myself to look at the man in passing I hate him so much. It's ridiculous, I can't explain it, it's like I'm connected to him through my hatred of him, but I hardly know the guy. Why is that?'

'Trevan, you say?' Old Doryty said slowly. 'It's a good question and no mistake,' she replied in her sweet singsong voice. 'Have you considered discussing the matter with young Andrew yourself?'

'What, you mean just go right up to him and tell him my madman ravings? How I dream of him every night? Tell him that I hate him because of those dreams? Tell him how scared I am to sleep because of him?' He stopped talking, realising he was ranting again. He was relieved that Miss Doryty didn't judge him, she simply gave him a kindly look and squeezed his hand comfortingly.

'Hate him, do you? Now that's a strong emotion to be having just because of a dream.' She paused for a moment

*The Cursed Shore*

as if in deep thought, then added with a smile and a twinkle in her eye, 'or is it?'

A wave of relief swept over Steven, she had not laughed or belittled his feelings or suggest he needed to see a doctor. He could tell that she knew something of what he was experiencing, he had been right to have shared his problems with her, she had listened, she understood and more importantly, she believed him.

'So, you think Trevan has something to do with my nightmares too?' he asked. 'What is it about him that affects me like this? It doesn't make any sense.' He breathed out long and slow, sat back into the chair and waited for Doryty to tell him her story.

'Not just him, more them, yes, that would be more accurate. His kin, against your kin, you know that much from the dream. Why don't you go and have a little talk with him, my dear? See if it makes you feel any different, get to know him, see if he is anything like the Trevan of the past. Then come back and tell me all about it, I'd like to know what he says.'

She gave him the comforting hand squeeze again, but Steven had been hoping for more.

'Now then,' she said smiling sweetly at him, 'how about that tea and cake?'

As she shuffled off to the small kitchen, Steven gently placed the calico cat back on the floor and took the opportunity for a small tour of the unusual room. Most of the bottles on the shelves appeared to contain herbs and resins. He even recognised some of the Latin names scrawled on to the bottle labels. He pushed some aside to see what was at the back; he was disappointed not to see Eye of Newt or Toe of Frog, although there was a small jar proclaiming to contain Dragons' Blood. The cat mewed at him and jumped on one of the shelves by the window threatening to knock the contents off. Steven quickly replaced her on the floor and straightened the wobbling bottles. He moved a few to make them safer and found himself looking at a small cloth figure of a man. It was lying on the shelf wrapped in what looked like a piece of torn sheet. He was pleased to see there were no pins or such like sticking out of it, just a single dark hair wrapped around its blank face.

Hearing Doryty returning he quickly moved the bottles back to hide the strange object. No doubt, that would be finding its way into the cardboard box to be thrown out with the rest of Marjory's occult trappings. He quickly sat down again as Doryty came in with the pot of steaming tea and a scrumptious-looking Victoria sponge cake all laid out on a pretty tray.

She gave him a curious look as she set it down on the small table and he smiled back with what he hoped was his best winning smile, one that he hoped did not say, yes, I was poking around your shelves whilst you weren't looking.

It wouldn't do to lose her trust now he had found an ally. However, she just smiled back at him and began pouring the tea and turning from the previous conversation to chitchat about the weather again and the local news, whilst he returned to fending off the affections of the cat, most of whom he now seemed to be wearing on his trousers. It was clear nothing more was going to happen here until he brought her news of his meeting with Trevan.

# CHAPTER 11

It was 6 a.m. when Steven crawled once more from the watery grave of his nightmare onto the soft bedroom carpet and waited for the gasping and groaning to subside and for his brain to find its way back to the 21$^{st}$ century. When his awareness returned, he wondered why it was still dark outside and where the wailing sound was coming from. A flash of lightning illuminated the bedroom, quickly followed by a crash of thunder exploding outside. A storm then, and almost overhead too. The sound of the wind blowing through the air vents gave it a haunting mournful wail that matched Steven's mood perfectly.

Cursing his luck, he climbed to his feet and staggered downstairs into the living room, bumping off the small doorframe as usual on his way in. He grimaced that the cottage was better designed for little old ladies than a full-grown man.

How much sleep had he managed this time he wondered? The last time he looked at the bedside clock it had been 3 a.m. and he had lain awake for a long time after that, too scared to give into the sleep he craved, knowing what awaited him if he did.

Another crash of thunder and the wind blew harder bellowing down the chimney and stirring the ashes in the wood burner. In the sunshine, the cottage was quaint and charming, but in weather like this, it felt claustrophobic and vulnerable. Steven assured himself that despite all the rattling and groaning of timbers the cottage had no doubt survived countless storms over the years and was good enough to endure countless more. The rain pounded on the roof and threw itself against the windows and door as if demanding to be let in. Steven huddled into the sofa and hugged his hot coffee mug.

He switched on the TV to take his mind from last night's nightmare and this morning's storm only to be dismayed when he was greeted by an enthusiastic face retelling 'the story of Aglets Cove so far.' The reporter referred to it as the Cursed Shore, the title he had given his own intended book on the subject. Bloody typical. He would have to think of another title now, that is, if he ever had the energy to write the damn thing. He was sure the general public were getting tired of hearing about bodies being washed up on a remote Cornish beach anyway. He knew he was.

It would be more newsworthy if a serial killer was thought to be at large but despite his own thoughts on the matter, they had all been declared accidental drownings. It had just been signed off as a mysterious coincidence. How convenient. Steven wondered about the bruising on the wrists of the victims he had the misfortune to see. He had never seen or heard these mentioned by anyone else, but they *had* been on that body, he had seen them with his own eyes.

He turned the TV off and made himself another mug of strong coffee. It always took more than one to make him feel remotely human again. He considered checking online for any conspiracy stories about the cove. Maybe there would be something on YouTube. He half hoped someone else had discovered the real curse too and maybe shared his nightmares. He might not be alone in this, and if there were others, then maybe he wasn't going insane.

He heard the chink of milk bottles being placed on his doorstep and admired the milkman for venturing out in such a storm. He envied the village folk going about their daily business as if no amount of bodies washed up on the beach could change their lives. The bodies on the beach were a concern for the Cornish tourist industry in the area

*The Cursed Shore*

and a source of gossip and speculation to everyone else, yet none of it seemed to bother the residents of Aglets Cove.

Steven though, could not even remember being so carefree. His existence was dominated by trying to stay awake and functioning whilst craving the sleep that he dreaded. It was a torturous existence made worse for seemingly being the only one affected.

He put the empty coffee mug on the counter. He was no more awake than the moment he had staggered out of bed. Maybe a couple more hours, he thought. Once the storm had passed, he would be able sleep easier. He wouldn't be fit for anything today if he didn't get a couple more hours in.

Standing in the small bedroom once more, Steven looked at his bed and hated it. He hated the plump latex pillow in its cool cotton pillowcase. He hated the extra-large duvet and the way he could snuggle into it and feel like he was lost in a protective embrace. He looked at the bed and knew it for the lie that it was. As soon as it lured him in into its soothing caress, sleep would overcome him and then it would become his torture chamber. The duvet would become the suffocating waves, the soft mattress, and the shifting sand beneath him. It would hold him there in its clutches until his dream-self died once more. Sighing he turned around and went back downstairs, maybe another coffee would be a better idea he thought.

By 10 a.m. a coffee fuelled Steven stood outside Constable Trevan's neatly laid out garden with its white picket fence and straight path to the door. Before opening the garden gate, Steven took a deep breath, and allowed himself a moment to enjoy that just after the rain smell and let it relax his tense muscles. He still wasn't sure what he would say to Constable Trevan once he was inside or how to say it without sounding completely bonkers. This was the 21st

*Ellen Hiller*

century for god's sake and here he was about to discuss the probability of an ancient curse killing people, with a police officer. Going to get filed under nutter for sure, he thought. Why on earth had he let Doryty talk him into this?

Steven sighed to himself as he swung open the little gate and was startled to see Trevan, already at the door, waiting for him, a wry smile on his face.

Steven cleared his throat nervously.

'Hello,' he said as cheerily as he could, not manic cheery just pleasant cheery he hoped. Ah shit he was already over thinking this. 'Lovely garden,' he added, pretending to be interested in the small dripping wet shrubs bordering the path.

'Hang on, why are there bottles buried in it?' Lining the path on both sides were a row of half buried glass bottles. Steven was wondering if it was supposed to be artistic, or maybe an old Cornish custom he was yet to hear about, but they appeared to be just ordinary plain glass bottles with corks in.

Trevan grinned at him and pulled one of the bottles from the ground so Steven could take a better look. Inside the scratched and dirty glass was an assortment of nails and rusted pins, what looked to be toenail clippings and plant debris floating in what Steven thought looked like…

'Is that piss in there?' Steven asked, stepping back from the bottle not trying to hide his distaste for the constable's choice in garden ornaments. Trevan laughed, obviously enjoying his little party trick.

'Yep,' he said, 'witches piss,' and he laughed again. 'They are witches bottles made to protect against witches spells and the like. Keeps them and their meddling away. These are ancient, been here longer than even my grandma has been alive, and that's a long time.' He laughed again; Steven was beginning to feel uncomfortable with the laughing.

'And you just leave them in there?' Steven asked fearing he knew the answer but hoped it not to be so.

*The Cursed Shore*

'Never know when you might need protection from a witch,' Trevan replied, giving Steven a knowing wink. Steven was growing uneasy, did the man know something, and did he know about their historical connection?

'So, you believe in all this occult stuff then?' Steven said.

Despite everything that was happening around him, from his nightmares and the dead bodies to a police constable standing in front of him holding a bottle of witch's piss, Steven still had a hard time accepting any of it. He wished more than anything for someone to hand him a pill and say, 'here take this and all this silly stuff will all go away.'

Trevan stopped and raised his head as if pondering the question carefully before replying. 'Historically,' he said, 'the occult, evil, witches, demons and such were always taken very seriously. Why do you think that stopped?'

'Because people were ignorant then,' Steven replied confidently, 'and now we are educated we know better.'

'Do we though?' Trevan said. 'Maybe it's easier to believe that evil does not exist in a modern world, but what if by not believing, evil finds a niche, a way to get in? If people stop believing maybe they are easier to corrupt, and how can you protect yourself from evil if you don't believe it's there?'

'What evil do *you* know about, Mr Trevan?' Steven asked donning his reporter's stance. Was it really going to be this easy he wondered trying hard to act casual and not grin like he was about to get what he came here for?

Constable Trevan laughed. 'Just repeating what me old gran said when she told me about the bottles,' then he turned to enter the house, beckoning Steven to join him. Steven tried not to sigh or show his disappointment; maybe he had come on too strong and overplayed his hand.

As they stepped over the threshold, the constable reached up and touched a stone that was hanging above the door, it had a hole through which the tattered string which suspended it was tied.

'Hag stone,' Trevan said to Steven as if he would understand. Steven thought of the action as almost instinctual, something the man had done all his life without question. No doubt, it was another charm, something else to protect the Trevans, something to keep them from justice.

An unbidden thought snarled through his mind, He saw Constable Trevan standing on the worn stone steps that led to the beach, a loaded musket pointed in his direction. A hot surge of anger run through Steven's veins and with it came a distant wailing from the direction of the beach. Just the wind he told himself, taking a deep breath to quell his anger, and followed the man into his house.

'So, Constable Trevan,' Steven began once they were settled in the small living room.

'Please call me Andrew,' Trevan said.

'Thank you, Andrew. I have been interviewing some of the residents of the village concerning the recent deaths at the cove. Can you tell me your opinion on the matter?'

Andrew Trevan gave Steven a deadpan serious look and replied, 'I'm afraid I can't discuss police business.'

'Well,' continued Steven, 'I thought now that they have been declared accidental deaths you would be free to comment.'

Steven put his notebook down.

'It can be off record if you like,' he said. 'I'd just like to hear your opinion.'

'Sorry,' said Trevan, although Steven thought he didn't look it. 'Still can't comment on it.'

'Okay, Andrew,' said Steven, yet to be defeated, 'what can you tell me about this village and your family's place in it? I hear the Trevans go back a long way.'

Andrew Trevan gave that wry smile again, and it stirred the embers of Steven's simmering anger, he forced the feeling down once more and tried to maintain a

*The Cursed Shore*

professional composure. Not that it helped, Trevan obviously wasn't going to give anything away.

'We are a very private family,' Trevan said. 'I intend to keep it that way, no offence, I know you are just doing your job.' Steven was exasperated. What was the point of Doryty sending him here he wondered? Then the constable threw the ball into his court. 'I believe your family have roots here too, Steven, I'm sure you have your own stories to tell.'

Steven was silent for a moment. Was Trevan being sarcastic or was he toying with him? He was sure the man knew the information he wanted and was being deliberately evasive.

'My parents moved away a long time ago, and they died a few years back. I only moved back here when I inherited the cottage from my grandma. I'm not sure if I can claim to have roots here personally. With my grandma gone, I am the last of the Aglets Cove Pearn's so there is no one left to ask I'm afraid.'

'Sorry to hear that about your folks, mate,' Trevan answered.

So, they were mates now, were they? Steven didn't think so.

'Don't be,' Steven said. 'Car crash, long time ago,' he shrugged back. And that was it, nothing else but small talk and village gossip and stuff on the news that did not contain dead bodies on beaches.

Despite the cold start, Trevan was quite chatty and amiable. Steven did his best to appear the same, and when he made his excuses to leave, Trevan patted him on the back and said he hoped to see him again soon. Steven tried not to shudder at the touch, he knew there was no reason for him to feel that way, but he could not help or control it.

'Yeah, same here,' he said as cheerfully as he could manage, and he walked back down the path through the avenue of witch's bottles as Trevan stood at the door and waved him off.

*Ellen Hiller*

'Hey, would you like to take a bottle or two with you?' Trevan called, gesturing to the bottles. 'Never know when you could use some witch protection.'

Steven tried not to grimace as he politely declined and imagined Trevan smirking at him as he walked back down the lane.

Doryty's home was just a few cottages along the way so Steven decided not to wait to tell her how the visit went.

Steven followed Doryty into the strange sitting room once more and noticed that despite Doryty saying she was clearing her sister's stuff out; the dusty shelves were still lined with their dusty bottles and bowls. He smiled knowingly, his own cottage was still filled with Nan's furniture and ornaments, such things take time. Luckily, the cat was somewhere else today, so he relaxed as he sank into the chair and told Doryty what had occurred between himself and Trevan. Doryty appeared less than happy with the conversational non-event.

'… and when I was leaving, Trevan had the cheek to ask me if I wanted a couple of the gross witch's bottles for my garden,' Steven said.

Doryty gripped the arm of the chair with a bony hand.

'And you said no, of course?' she said.

'Of course, I said no. Filthy things, why would I want them?'

'Good.' Doryty looked visibly relieved. 'Absolutely right, horrid filthy things they are. I'll put the kettle on.'

Steven smiled after her as she shuffled off into the kitchen. She was such a dear old thing, looking out for him just as his nan would have.

# CHAPTER 12

Andrew Trevan waved Steven goodbye then closed the door firmly. He rested his forehead against the wood and forced himself to relax. He was sure that there was more to the man's visit than just a journalist asking him the same questions as he was with all the village folk. You don't just knock on the door of a policeman's home and expect information about an ongoing investigation. Andrew was worried Steven knew more than he was letting on; the man had seemed on edge, something was off, but Andrew just couldn't put his finger on it. The last thing he needed was a nosey journalist on his case.

On the other hand, he thought, maybe I'm being paranoid. Apparently, Steven lived in the village now and what's more, he was going out with Sandra. He turned his nose up at that thought, but they had friends in common now, so maybe the man was just being friendly, neighbourly.

Andrew walked into the living room cursing himself for having been so friendly to the guy when he had first met him on the beach, it had obviously just encouraged the man to want to make it personal.

He poured himself a drink and considered his options. Could he use the reporter in some way? Sandra had informed him that he was friendly with Doryty and after all, a spy in that particular camp would be a useful tool to have. But then it was one that could just as easily work both ways. For all he knew it was Doryty that sent him over here in the first place.

Sandra seemed to think Steven was trustworthy, but she was dating the guy, so of course she would say that. There was too much at stake here for guesswork. Not for the first time Andrew wished he had Marjory to talk to. She would have known what to do, she always did. She was the glue that bound everything together and without her, it was all falling apart.

He missed Marjory so much, not only because of her skills when working the craft but also for the way she was, for who she was. She was so strong, never doubting herself or those around her. She taught, she guided and most of all, she inspired. She had helped his younger awkward self to come to terms with who he was until he found his own way.

Then there was her personality, the flamboyant, colourful, decadent Marjory, so unlike her sour-faced dour sister. When you saw Marjory, the last thing you would have thought was witch.

He remembered her long grey hair that she usually wore in a large bun, clasped in place with a huge glittering hair clip. However, when she was working the craft, when she stood at the bonfire site and performed the ritual, then it was unbound and ruled by the wind, echoing the freedom of her spirit.

Andrew never noticed the lines and wrinkles that time had painted on Marjory's face. To him she was timeless, maid, mother and crone personified, she was all three at once.

How could a spirit such as hers be taken away from the world by an earthly illness? Surely, death could not bind someone like her, he thought. She may be buried in the old churchyard, but he refused to believe that she was gone forever from his life.

Andrew sighed and put his empty glass on the coffee table. He would just have to work harder, try to be more like her and get better. And he had to hope that the next body didn't wash up in the cove. Too many questions were already being asked and everyone wanted to solve the mystery. He fumbled absently with the small leather pouch which was fastened around his neck. Steven Pearn, he decided, could be trusted as much as Doryty was and if that upset Sandra then so be it.

# CHAPTER 13

The wind rattled the ropes against the mast and tugged at the securely tied sail as if trying to loosen it and hasten their journey. Donald looked up to triple check that everything was in order, it was, of course. He was an experienced sailor, a fact that he never tired of telling everyone. He always did everything right and by the book and it had kept him in good stead for all his time at sea, which amounted to a great deal of his life.

This trip, however, was the first he had taken Mavis along with him. It had seemed logical at first, sailing down to Cornwall for a holiday to visit her family instead of driving there. Now that he was retired, the journey could take as long as it needed to, he could just relax and enjoy the view, even if it did mean sharing it with his wife. Donald wished he could live on the boat with nothing but the endless sea for company, relying on his wits and endless knowledge to survive. Doing what he wanted, when he wanted, and not having to answer to anything, especially a nagging wife.

Mavis hated sailing, although he had often wondered if that was just her excuse so that she didn't have to spend much time with him, especially since he had retired. He had been surprised when she had agreed to sailing down the coast for their holidays, and he hoped she wouldn't enjoy the experience too much.

The wooden steps to the cabin creaked and Donald tried not to grimace as Mavis stepped up beside him.

*The Cursed Shore*

'Ah Mavis, you must have read my mind I was just thinking about you, come up and join me dear, it's so nice having you here spoiling me,' he lied.

Mavis had appeared from the galley with two steaming mugs of coffee. Oh no, she thought, I hope he doesn't want me to stay and chat. She did her best to force a smile.

'Oh, I'm really enjoying being here,' Mavis lied. 'I had no idea what I've been missing out on all these years.' Mavis really did not want to stay and chat, there was a racy romance novel waiting for her below decks and she couldn't wait to get back to it. 'Well I don't want to get in the way up here, so I'll be off,' she cringed as she said it, hoping he wouldn't look too disappointed. Donald tried not to show the relief he felt as he took his coffee and she scuttled back down the wooden steps back to the cabin.

How long could they keep this up? Mavis wondered. They could hardly avoid each other on a boat this size. Next time she vowed to herself, she would take the train.

It was only early evening, but she got ready for bed anyway, snuggling up with her book was the best way to pass time on what seemed like an endless voyage. If Donald ever tore himself away from the business end of the boat, she could pretend to be asleep. She looked out of the small porthole at the grey lifeless sea; thank god, they would be in Padstow by lunchtime tomorrow she thought as she flipped over the next page in her book.

The wind grew stronger and Donald turned the radio on to catch the latest shipping forecast and listened to the familiar and comforting voice telling him the weather was … fair with good visibility … seas slight or moderate … the wind variable, mainly northeast, three or four. Everything was fine, just as Donald had predicted. He checked his watch; it was still quite early, so he picked up his newspaper and decided to read it all over again. By the time he finished he could be sure Mavis was asleep and

73

*Ellen Hiller*

snoring, and then he would sneak in and grab some sleep himself before setting sail to Padstow in the morning.

Hours later and Donald opened his eyes wondering what had woken him. He looked at his watch; 3 a.m. not time to get up yet. He turned over, pulled the duvet over his head, closed his eyes again, and waited for sleep to reclaim him once more. It was no good however; he could not relax, without knowing why he was awake. His instincts told him he should go topside and recheck everything was in order even though everything was well and truly checked before he went to bed. Sill, one more time wouldn't hurt would it. Better to be safe than sorry, something might have come adrift in the night. Always best to be sure.

Decision made, Donald jumped out of bed, no longer caring about his lost sleep. There was enough moonlight seeping through the cabin porthole to see by and he carefully slipped his feet into his deck shoes, pulled his jumper over his pyjamas, and quietly tiptoed out. Waking the loudly snoring Mavis was the last thing he wanted to do. She would only start to worry then get into a flap over nothing, and besides what if she wanted to help? That would be unthinkable.

He climbed up the wooden steps to the wheelhouse, this part of the yacht was covered with a tarpaulin canopy making it that much colder than below decks. Donald reached for his coat that was hanging over the back of a chair but stopped halfway, something really was wrong and ringing alarm bells with his sense of order.

From the starboard window, he could see cliffs and a beach. Somehow, the anchor must have dislodged at some point in the night leaving the boat to drift towards the shoreline. He ran to check it, worse than just being dislodged, it was gone. Its chain now hung uselessly down the side of the vessel. How the hell could that have happened? There had been no storm, not even rough waves. He cursed his luck but there was no time to look

*The Cursed Shore*

for answers now. They were drifting in fast and he guessed the boat must be caught in a strong current that was pulling them into dangerous water.

Donald tried to start the engine, nothing; he tried again, still nothing. This is ridiculous, he thought, as the third try was just as fruitless, everything was fine just a few hours ago, and we were miles offshore, it made no sense at all. Panic started to replace his cold efficiency as he assessed the situation. The anchor was gone, the engine wasn't working, and they were heading, unpowered, into a cove with the possibility of large rocks below the surface water as was common in this area. He turned on the radio, time to call the coastguard he thought, but his heart sank when it was as dead as the engine.

'Something wrong, dear?' came the sound of Mavis's voice as she climbed the steps to the wheelhouse 'Oh, are we are nearly there already? That's good,' Mavis yawned as she looked out of the window. 'You were running about up here so much you woke me.'

'You stupid cow!' Donald shouted. He had never shouted at her before, even though he had to constantly bite down on his lip to stop himself from doing so. The shouting was good though. Therapeutic even, and went a considerable way to relieving his stress, so he continued. 'Can't you see what's happening? You had better start praying this engine starts soon, or it's the end of the boat, the holiday and maybe even the end of us.'

Mavis was tempted to remark that because of the way he was behaving that didn't seem like such a bad thing right now, but she resisted. She was still half-asleep, and the full impact of their plight had not hit her yet, but she did feel like something was wrong, not with the boat though, or Donald's ranting, there was something beyond that, something about the unnatural darkness of the cove they were heading into. A dread fear seeped into her along with the cold and she thought that maybe she was still asleep and that this was going to be a nightmare. She moved closer to Donald.

'I don't like this, not at all.' She trembled as she said it and reached for Donald's hand, needing to steady herself. 'Well I'm not exactly over the moon about it myself,' he cut back at her, but when he saw how frightened she looked he wished he could say something more comforting. He paused for a moment and patted her hand, hoping to find the reassuring words that wouldn't come.

Donald turned the key one more time and this time the engine spluttered into life. 'Oh, thank you, thank you,' he cried to no one in particular. As he put the boat into reverse and started to steer away from the cove, he was further relieved to hear the radio crackle, order was beginning to be restored at last.

'Mavis, get on the radio, quick, we still might need some help here.'

Mavis didn't move. 'The radio, quickly, dear,' he tried to sound calmer than he was, hoping to coax her along. Still she did not move, instead she stared mortified out of the window at the hand that had appeared on the rail outside. Another hand appeared beside it, pale and dripping wet, its tattered flesh hanging from skeletal fingers. Mavis watched unable to move, she tried to shout, to get Donald's attention, but all that happened was a slight squeak, another second slowly passed, then the thing was aboard.

Mavis tried to scream but again all that came out was a muted squeak. She tried to step back, but her legs were jelly and not responding. All she could do was watch as her brain frantically tried to make sense of what her eyes were seeing.

The man now standing on the deck looked like he had stepped out of a history book. He was tall and unkempt, his face weather-beaten and scarred with the jawbone half exposed through rotten flesh the other half hidden by the long, wet hair that clung to it. His eyes were dull and

*The Cursed Shore*

expressionless, and they were fixed on hers. He moved slowly forwards, his muscular frame showing under the wet clothing, his naked feet were soundless on the wooden decking.

Mavis's head was muzzy, her ears were ringing, and she could feel the vomit rising in her throat. Where was Donald? Why wasn't he doing anything? Faintly she heard his voice, detached and unreal; he was on the radio calling for help. She thought she heard him say 'no immediate danger.' What was he talking about, hadn't he seen what was standing in front of her? Was he blind?

The sky was getting brighter as the dawn approached and Mavis, still transfixed on the man watched as he slowly walked towards her. She prayed he would fade away along with the darkness, because that's how ghosts and nightmares worked wasn't it? Everything was supposed to be safe and normal during the day.

Unfortunately, the dawn light only improved her vision; she could now see a second pair of hands on the rail outside. Once more, she tried to scream, forcing a muted gurgle from her throat. Then as if a spell over her had broken Mavis lurched forwards screaming and howling like a banshee.

Donald spun round to face her.

'For god's sake, woman, what's the matter with you? Can't you see I'm trying ...' but his words trailed into nothing as he stared in disbelief at the sight of his wife running backwards out of the cabin and onto the deck. Her movement was strange and jerky; reminiscent of a macabre puppet show he had seen in Poland on another trip. Then she just slid over the side of the yacht; she didn't fall, she slid, almost as if some invisible force was pulling her.

Donald rushed out on deck ready to jump in and save her, clearly, he thought, she was having some kind of seizure no doubt brought on by the stress of their situation. Kicking off his deck shoes, he looked over the side of the boat, expecting to see her thrashing about in the water, but the surf was calm and unbroken. He dived in anyway, his eyes wide open, scanning beneath the surface for a sign of her, but there was nothing. Donald knew there was no use looking anymore; she had obviously been caught in a current and being pulled to who knows where on the whim of the tide. He hoped, sincerely, that she would wash up alive and well in the cove, although he knew this was unlikely as Mavis was not much of a swimmer.

As he climbed back aboard, he tried not to feel too relieved about not having to spend the holiday with his wife's quaint Cornish family, then put on his most concerned voice as he went back to the radio to call in this latest turn of events.

# CHAPTER 14

Steven awoke with a gasp and stared at the ceiling waiting for his thoughts to return to normal. The nightmare was fading quickly but the wailing sound of the chanted curse was still ringing in his ears. He rubbed them, trying to get them back to the present day. Worryingly he could still hear the faint singsong sounds somewhere in the distance, faint but distinctive.

He lay there for a while trying to get back to sleep, but sleep refused to come, and the wailing curse did not leave him. As he listened to it, bewildered, Steven realised the sound had a direction. He got up and opened the bedroom window and the sound became louder. His heart started to thump wildly in his chest and his hand on the window latch began to tremble.

His nightmare had now intruded into his waking hours.

Steven quickly dressed, fuelled by adrenalin, and without thinking about what he was going to do when he got there, he set out into the night to follow the eerie chant.

He had half expected the sound to have disappeared when he opened the front door, but it was still there, tauntingly real. Steven could tell that the sound was being carried on the wind that blew down from the cliff path and he set out to follow it.

There was also the smell of wood smoke in the air, unlikely to be from a wood burner in the middle of a summer's night he thought, someone had a fire lit.

Just as he had done as a child, Steven climbed the steep grassy banks that took him out of the village road and along the dirt track at the edge of the cliffs. The chant neither stopped nor wavered. It was a constant noise against the background of the gentle sea. It sometimes gathered intensity, sometimes it was quieter, so much so that he had to strain to hear it, but it never stopped.

An outcrop of rocks jutting out from the side of the path hid the view up ahead and he ran until he was past it, then he could see firelight in the distance. This must be his destination; a thrill of excitement ran through him and he quickened his pace.

As he got closer, the chanting got louder; he could see the dancing flames of a large bonfire and the figures of several people standing around it. At first, he imagined they would be dancing wildly to the tune of the curse but on closer inspection, the figures were standing still in a circle around the fire as they sang the ancient words.

Steven stopped to catch his breath and consider his options. Despite his curiosity, and a need to know who these people were, he wondered if it was wise to get any closer, but if he didn't, he would regret it, maybe there wouldn't be another chance. As he stood there summoning the courage to go on, he became aware that he could hear the chant coming from a second direction, this time against the wind and emanating from the beach below.

The path had taken him to the edge of the cove and the bonfire was directly above the cliff wall that held the old iron mooring ring, the thought of it made him physically shudder. The second chant was coming from the beach below the bonfire, however there was not a matching bonfire, and in the dark, he was unable to see if anyone was down there.

He took a few steps backwards; fear was getting the better of his curiosity and he crouched down amongst the hawthorn bushes in case they spotted him. The chant was louder now, never missing a beat, the tune from his nightmares so familiar he had to force himself not to hum along. Its ancient melody resonating from the cliff-top and the beach in unison. Then abruptly the chanting stopped

*The Cursed Shore*

and all that could be heard in the darkness of the night was the gentle slosh of the sea as the tide rolled in.

Steven instinctively turned on his heel and ran back down the path. He wasn't sure if he had been spotted or if the night's event had just reached a natural conclusion, but either way he was sure he didn't want to find out.

As he ran, he knew he was running from the very people who could answer all his questions, maybe even help him with his nightmares, explain his bizarre predicament. However, they could just as easily be the ones who were responsible for his predicament. If that was the case, how much danger was he in if they caught him spying on them? What if they were sacrificing someone in the ritual and there would be another body on the beach tomorrow?

He was in over his head here and alone; this was something he would have to discuss with Doryty tomorrow, although if she had known what was going on here, surely, she would have told him already, unless maybe she thought she was protecting him.

By the time Steven reached home, he was exhausted and gasping for breath. He burst into the cottage, double locking the door behind him, and crouched down beside the hallway window to see if he had been followed. It seemed like hours had passed when he eventually heard footsteps coming down the lane from the direction of the cliff path. He held his breath and watched, frozen to the spot as a group of robed people walked past the cottage. One of them stopped as they passed the window. Steven ducked down hoping he had not been seen. Then the footsteps sounded again as the person caught up with the rest of the group. Steven breathed again, his heart racing, they had to be the same group from the clifftop bonfire. He knew he should open the door and confront them, but all he could do was sit shivering in fear and hoping that they did not come back and knock.

The footsteps eventually faded into the distance and he waited until they could no longer be heard before letting out a huge sigh of relief. Then cursed himself for his cowardice.

# CHAPTER 15

The next morning, Steven waved at Andrew Trevan from his car as he passed him in the lane. The police constable was busy loading the boot of his car with branches from a felled tree. Good bonfire material, Steven thought, and his heart froze. The constable gave Steven a cheery smile and waved back as the car sped passed him.

He was on his way to the office to do some ordinary everyday work and to try to remember what it was to lead a normal uneventful life but instead he found himself suspicious of everyone he passed. Could that young girl with the pushchair have been up on the clifftop last night? Did she just give him a sideways glance as he passed? Or that man over there; Steven was sure he was just pretending to look in the shop window. Maybe he was watching Steven in its reflection. Then there was the sweet old woman from the corner shop where he bought his morning paper, something about the way she looked at him as she gave him his change. Any of them could have been round that bonfire, or none of them at all and he was turning into a paranoid madman.

Steven cursed himself for not getting close enough last night to see their faces. He wondered if the bonfire was a regular thing, every night maybe, to induce his nightmares. Maybe last night had been a special occasion. He knew it wasn't the anniversary of the smugglers' demise, but it could have been another significant date. The thought of the bodies being washed up on the beach being some sort of ritual sacrifice occurred to him, and he had to pull into a layby to steady his breathing. He was thinking worst-case

*The Cursed Shore*

scenarios, he knew that. He also knew he was only doing that to excuse his running away last night. But what if these people really did have something to do with the recent deaths? Until now, he had just been thinking of his own plight, but what of the bodies on the beach, and their bizarre connection to the past? He knew nothing about magic or its power, or even if he believed in it, despite all the apparent evidence to the contrary. However, there was no ignoring the strange things that were happening here, maybe inheriting Nan's cottage wasn't the blessing he thought it was.

Something else to ask old Doryty, Steven thought. Her sister had clearly been a witch, she would know. He would have laughed at the very idea of witches and curses a few weeks back. Nothing was funny anymore.

The familiarity of the *Recorder's* old dilapidated office was comforting. Steven could count the days he'd spent there on one hand but, even so, the smell of old papers and coffee reminded him of normality, and he breathed it all in as if it were the elixir of life. As he walked to his desk, he staggered, and had to grab a chair for support, and looked up hoping no one had seen him only to find his editor giving him a concerned look.

Steven blushed and stuttered an explanation

'Need sleep,' he said, 'not been able to sleep lately, if I could just get one good night's sleep, I'd be fine.'

John, his editor, did not look convinced and Steven waited for the harsh words to come, no doubt accusing him of being drunk and not up to the job, but they did not come. As he looked up from his desk, John was already walking back to his office shaking his head.

The *West Coast Recorder* was a small-time local newspaper so, fuelled with coffee, Steven was able to catch up on his work without paying much attention. Then, after putting one sheet of paper in the finished pile revealed another, until now, unseen beneath it. John must have left it here for him, there was no note attached, nothing to make it special except that as he looked at it, Steven found his stomach churning and his breath quickening. It was the coroner's report on the first body. A picture outline of a man with lines pointing out where various marks had been found, or bits of flesh missing. It was immediately apparent that there were no lines pointing to the wrists. No mention of the bruising that had to be from some form of restraint. He skimmed over the short paragraphs looking for the missing evidence. Nothing.

At the bottom of the page, cause of death was listed as accidental death by drowning. Steven stared at the report as if he could will the missing details there. He thought back to the gruesome sight of the body on the beach. Had he imagined the marks? He realised that no one else had mentioned them. Could it all have been part of the awful hallucination he had experienced that day? This would explain the accidental death verdict, and why the major media had never shown any interest. But what if he hadn't imagined the marks, and someone had falsified the records? That would be a whole new can of worms.

He tried ringing the coroner's office but there was no one there to take his call so he left a message detailing his concerns about the missing marks, then instantly regretted it. They would no doubt laugh at this small-town reporter and his over-active imagination. Steven laid the report back down, and once more questioned own sanity, something he was doing far too often lately.

It was approaching lunchtime, and as he was up to date on all the mundane work, Steven was able to escape to his car for a quiet think or maybe even a quick nap in the car park. He had plans for tonight and sleep wasn't part of those plans.

Two hours later, and Steven was woken by his editor banging on his car window. He opened his eyes with no memory of a dream or nightmare. John must have wondered why he looked so cheerful as he sleepily unwound the passenger-side window.

*The Cursed Shore*

'You know you could just go home and go to bed, don't you?' John said.

Steven just shrugged and started the car, there was no point even trying to explain.

'Don't rush off just yet,' John said with a large grin on his face. 'Guess what just washed up in the cove?'

Steven groaned. 'Not another one?'

'Yep, a woman this time, yet to be identified but there was apparently a man, or woman rather, overboard incident in the early hours of the morning, at the mouth of the cove no less. Probably her.'

'How come I'm only hearing about this now?'

'Thought you could do with a rest, mate, obviously just another coincidence, but do you mind taking a look?'

'No need,' Steven replied wearily. 'Might as well just wait for the official report and see their version of events.'

John gave him a curious look, but Steven couldn't be bothered to explain. He put the engine in gear and started to pull away then stopped and asked, 'What was her name, surname, the woman that went overboard?'

'Sorry, mate, no idea yet.' John shrugged and walked off back to the office. Steven expected it to be an old name, a name with a historical connection to the cove, the name of a Revenue man.

# CHAPTER 16

'More cake, dear?' Doryty said. 'You look like you could do with building up.' Steven politely took the cake. There was always cake at Doryty's; she was becoming a surrogate grandmother as well as a confidant. If the visits kept up Steven was sure he would be building out rather than up.

As Doryty poured tea into little pottery mugs, he decided to rush in with the question.

'Doryty, your sister was a witch, wasn't she?' Doryty's tea pouring paused for a second before continuing.

'Yes, dearie, some would say that.'

The uncommitted response irritated Steven, but he hid it under a mask of politeness.

'So, do you know much about magic and stuff?' He gestured at the dusty shelves that were still full of their oddities. 'Did she share anything with you? You two must have been very close.' Once again, Doryty evaded the question, this time by asking one of her own.

'So, what's on your mind today, dear? Why all the witchy questions? Has another nightmare upset you?'

'Every sleeping moment is a nightmare,' he replied. 'And yes, they upset me. But last night a part of that nightmare came to life.'

Doryty frowned then reached over to give his hand a reassuring squeeze,

'In what way, dearie? Tell me everything,' she said. Soothed by her maternal concern Steven told Doryty about the bonfire above the beach whilst Doryty and the cat listened intently.

*The Cursed Shore*

When Steven had finished talking Doryty put down her now empty mug with great care. A deep frown had set on her face and when she spoke, there was a slight quiver in her voice.

'Whatever was going on up there, dearie, you were right to run away. Some people you don't want to be dealing with.'

'Who exactly?' Steven asked.

'Not sure as I know,' she replied. Her avoidance was getting tiresome, but Steven knew he had to be patient with her.

'I have my suspicions,' she continued. 'Friends of my sister maybe, but I won't accuse without being sure.'

Steven relaxed a little, she wasn't being evasive after all, she just wasn't jumping to conclusions. Although he was not getting the answers he needed, he was grateful as always that she was taking him seriously. When he was with Doryty, he didn't feel like a nutcase, and more importantly to him, he did not feel alone in all this mess.

'I will ask some discreet questions here and there,' she told him, giving him her usual reassuring squeeze of the hand. 'If it happens again, see if you can get close enough to see their faces. But be sneaky about it though. We don't want them knowing we are on to them.' She giggled at this for some reason.

Steven picked up the now cold mug of tea and drank it down. Another visit to Doryty and he was none the wiser but comforted at least and hopeful of some help.

He left Doryty's cottage and ambled down the leafy lane towards home, brushing off white cat hairs from his trousers as he went.

He had no work to do today, and the weather was fine. A perfect day for a little hike along the cliff path. It was late morning and there were just a few tourists ambling about. He was safe enough to go exploring up there without looking suspicious. It was a normal thing to do after all.

*Ellen Hiller*

The trek along the grassy path was quicker and easier in the daylight. He even stopped occasionally to admire the view. Rolling countryside to his right and to his left the rolling deep blue ocean. The sky was cloudless and the cries from the seagulls and the crash of waves bringing the smell of the sea on the breeze added to the ambiance of the scene. He had thought when he moved back to Nan's home as an adult Aglets Cove would have lost some of the charm it held from his childhood memories, but it never had. No matter what strange events occurred, or what the nightmares tried to do to him, he would never tire of its beauty.

As Steven walked on, the smell of wood smoke began to waft his way again as he neared the bonfire site. Last night he had thought it to be on the actual path; however, he could now see that it had been a few metres away in a field adjacent to the path. He made a mental note of his bearings, figuring it might be useful to find out who owns the land there. Then he hopped over the low stone wall and walked over to the scorched earth of the bonfire site and the still smouldering pile of ash. The whole area on the edge of the field looked dead and blackened and there were large piles of old ash next to the wall. There clearly had been many bonfires here over goodness knows how many years.

In the daylight, it all looked boringly normal, Steven wasn't sure what he'd been expecting, but it looked just like any other bonfire site. It could have easily been made by the farmer burning dead wood, nothing more sinister than just a common old bonfire.

He stood there, thinking back to last night, the chanting, and the menacing silhouettes of the circle of people who had been standing there. As his mind wandered back to the strange event, he realised he was staring at a shallow marking on the ground.

Steven crouched down to get a closer look. The shape looked almost runic with its straight lines and sharp edges,

*The Cursed Shore*

but it wasn't anything he recognised. He took his phone out of his pocket and took a photo, then noticed a second marking a little further along. This second one was looked less runic and looked more like an Egyptian cartouche. He took another photo, not just a random thing then, he thought, feeling pleased with himself, then looked for the next. He knew it would be there but still he caught his breath in wonder when he saw it. Then there was another, and then another.

There were six in total, circling the bonfire site. Each of the markings was different, but they had been a deliberate working, there was nothing random about the sharp edges and curved lines.

Steven was so elated he could have shouted in delight. Actual physical evidence of something sinister going on here. He couldn't wait to show Sandra, maybe now she would take him seriously. Not a dream this time, this was something that therapy could not fix.

After checking that there was nothing else to see, he pocketed his phone and headed home; smiling to himself as he went and not caring about the strange looks passers-by were giving him.

By the time Sandra arrived at his cottage, Steven was already two hours into an internet search of magical symbols that so far had not yielded any results. She looked over his shoulder, then at his phone as he recounted his story. As her eyes widened, and he felt like she was hearing him for the first time. That is until she remarked:

'There are lots of pagans in the area, it could be the site of a moot, an entirely innocent meeting.'

Steven slammed the lid of the laptop down in frustration.

'What about the chanting then, it matched my nightmares?'

'Maybe you dreamed that bit,' she answered, 'and can you even be sure it was the same tune as in your nightmare? You know memories can play tricks on you sometimes.'

Steven looked at her, his jaw dropping. What did it take to convince the woman he wondered? He remembered the cutting in the library that had said 'a hand came out of the sea and pulled him under'. If Sandra had seen that happening, she would probably swear it was an octopus that had pulled the man down. He wondered if she was totally lacking in imagination or just had a closed mind to anything out of the ordinary.

Sandra looked worried by his outburst, and Steven quickly calmed his temper and smiled at her innocence. Sandra was a down-to-earth, practical kind of girl, who could blame her for not understanding all this supernatural stuff.

'Sorry, love, you're right, I'm totally overthinking this stuff. Let's go and get a drink and a bite to eat.' Immediately the tension lifted, and her face brightened up again.

There was no use trying to involve her anymore, Steven realised. It would have been nice to have her on side, but at least she had her own ways to help him forget the nightmares for a while.

# CHAPTER 17

The cottage was dark and full of shadows and as Steven sat by his window a thrill of excitement tingled up his spine. He had set up a small table with coffee and snacks and was prepared to spend the whole night if need be scrutinising anyone who walked down the lane in the direction of the cliff path. He had a notebook balanced on his knee and a pen in hand ready to jot down descriptions or even better, names.

It was 11.30 p.m. and so far, he had seen nothing worth noting down, but he wasn't daunted, and anyway, it wasn't as if nights were for sleeping anymore. He had managed to snatch another hour on the sofa, and he would snatch another two or three when the sun came up tomorrow. That is how his sleep was managed these days. An hour here, two there, sometimes a whole morning and some of those snatched moments were blissfully without the nightmares. However, any sleep in the hours of darkness were guaranteed to see him drowning, so he didn't even bother to try.

An hour later as he stretched his arms, as much to alleviate the boredom as to stop them from seizing up, Steven heard the sound of several feet coming up the lane towards the cliff path, along with the low murmur of quietened speech. His heart started to beat wildly as he made sure that he was positioned to allow maximum view whilst being hidden by a large shrub in front of the window and the shadow it cast. He held his breath and waited, enjoying feeling more like the predator for once rather than the prey.

There were only six of them, it had seemed like there were more in front of the bonfire yesterday, and they were dressed in dark hooded robes. Steven swore under his breath; the hoods were large and gaping, causing the faces inside to be cast in shadow and unrecognisable. However, he was able to guess by the size difference of the figures that at least two of them were women, but that was all. He threw the notepad and pen down in frustration. There was no alternative but to follow them along the cliff path in the hope they removed the robes at some point in their ceremony.

He had hoped it wouldn't have come to this but knowing how his luck, or lack of it, panned out he was already dressed to fit the occasion. He pulled up the hood on his black sweatshirt, together with his black jeans and trainers he was sure he could blend in with the shadows if he was quiet enough. He could be sneaky too if he had to be, and he smiled as he remembered Doryty's words and girlish giggle. Taking a deep breath to steady his nerves he quietly opened the front door and stepped out into the night.

It was dark and moonless, and the air smelled vaguely of roses and the sea. The stars looked glorious studded against the midnight sky, and Steven couldn't help but take a moment to gaze at them in awe. However, all this beauty could not distract from the thudding in his chest and the new-found sense of purpose as he slowly crept along the lane.

He followed the group, just close enough not to lose them but still at a safe distance. If they turned and spotted him, there would be no innocent excuse for his being there. But he wasn't daunted at the prospect. His fear had turned to excitement, and he was relishing it, for the moment at least. He was taking control of his life at last,

*The Cursed Shore*

and it gave him a sense of power to be watching them from the shadows.

Steven watched the small robed party amble along the path and his confidence grew. With their hoods up they would have to turn around completely to see him, and this would give him enough warning to hide in the undergrowth at the side of the path.

They did not turn, however, or even slow their pace, and when they reached the spot above the mooring ring where the bonfire had been, they stopped and climbed over the low wall into the field beyond. Steven slowed his pace, he wanted to give them time to light their fire and be engrossed in the event before he was in full view of them. But the fire never happened.

He approached their part of the wall on all fours, hugging the side as close as he could so as not to be seen. From there he could hear anguished cursing and the striking of matches.

'Are you sure the wood isn't wet?' he heard a man's voice say.

'Of course, I'm sure,' came the hushed reply.

'Here, let me try,' a woman's voice this time.

'It's no good,' the first voice again, 'the newspaper isn't even taking.'

'Do we really need the fire? Can't we just do the marks and the ritual?' another voice asked. Then a familiar voice answered.

'Worth a try, a bonfire as such might not be needed; a candle could represent the fire element.'

'All very well but did anyone bring a candle?'

Steven didn't wait to hear the answer. He was already staggering back the way he had come, gasping for breath as his heart lurched trying to escape the confines of his chest via his throat and with nausea threatening to overwhelm him. The sound of Sandra's voice was still ringing in his ears.

*Ellen Hiller*

Safe in the cottage once more, whilst pacing the room, Steven tried to recall his conversations with Sandra regarding the curse. He tried to analyse her comments and her lack of any real concern. He remembered the night she wanted to make love on the beach beneath the stars. The thought sickened him now. He had felt watched there that night. Were her fellow conspirators the ones who were doing the watching? He could think of no other explanation.

His head was buzzing with ideas and conspiracies. He could hardly wait until morning when he could deliver this new information to Doryty. He wondered if she already had an inkling about Sandra. If ever he had mentioned his girlfriend, she had always been dismissive of her.

It occurred to him, as he came to terms with the night's events that he had not heard any chanting yet, despite knowing that they were still up there on the clifftop, trying their evil ritual without a fire. Maybe the wind was blowing in the opposite direction tonight. He opened the window a little to hear better, then quickly shut it again as he heard hushed voices and footsteps once more in the lane.

From behind the window, Steven looked on the small gathering as they walked past his cottage. One stopped outside his gate and turned to face the front door. It had to be Sandra he thought and ducked down in case she spotted him. As he sat crouched there, he wondered if he should straight up and confront her, right now, with her stood there in her robe. How could she even try to deny her involvement then? He went to the front door and hesitated for a moment longer as he calmed his temper, then decided to hell with the consequences and flung the door open dramatically.

Steven stood there, his heart pounding frantically in his chest as he prepared to vent his anger and injustices, only to see the group disappearing into the darkened lane. He was tempted to call after her, but with the exhalation of a deep breath he hadn't realised he was holding in, the moment had passed. What would he say? He rationally decided not to reveal his knowledge of her just yet and quietly shut the door again.

When the night was over and the sun rose again, Steven dared to take a fitful nap on the sofa, waking to the sound of his alarm at 10 a.m. He lay there unmoving for a while as he tried to mentally digest the last night's events. In the cold light of day and the sanity it brought with it, Steven was glad that he had not revealed himself to Sandra, in fact he felt quite smug about it. He now knew something that they did not. Trying to act natural around Sandra was going to be awkward, but he was sure he could pull off an innocent look as he told her he had seen her group heading towards the cliff path. It would be good to see her reaction.

His excitement was beginning to grow now as he wondered if she would confess all or act surprised. Once more, he welcomed feeling positive about something. He still didn't understand the how or the why. Nor did he want to accept the idea of witchcraft actually being a real thing and he wondered if Sandra had hypnotised him at some point without him realising it. Whatever the reason for her doing it, or even how it was being done, he knew someone was making his nightmares happen for whatever warped reason they might have. He also hoped his newfound knowledge was the key to making them stop.

First, he had to see Doryty. She would know what to do.

# CHAPTER 18

Andrew Trevan looked at the pile of wood in disgust. The others had decided to give up and go home. No bonfire, no ritual. He wondered if they took the whole thing seriously enough. Hadn't their previous failures been underlined enough? Failure meant someone had to pay the price, and that price was evident for all to see when the sea decided to bring it back home.

They had to get better, but he did not know what else he could do? The fire refusing to light was a new low. He bent down and inspected a few of the logs. As he had expected they were completely dry, and so was the kindling nestled in between them too, so why didn't it take? There was only one possible answer: Doryty.

He kicked about at the base of the woodpile looking for evidence, but he doubted if she would have left anything visible behind. He lit another match and held it against a small piece of wood, it fizzled and went out despite the fact there was no wind to take it. Taking his knife, he shaved a few curly wisps of wood from the end, as thin as paper, and then struck another match. As soon as the flame touched the wood, it fizzled out and died again, this time leaving a small plume of dark blue smoke with a tell-tale smell.

'Damn the woman!' he snarled, now he would have to find a counter spell to work against hers before tomorrow's ritual. At least Sandra had Marjory's book of shadows, he thought. He was confident that Marjory would have something written down for this very situation.

Not for the first time he realised just how unprepared they were to take this on themselves. Next time they would bring the spell book and a bag of supplies so that they would be able to counter anything Doryty threw at them there and then.

Giving up on the bonfire Andrew put his hood up and jogged along the path to catch the others up. When they left the cliff path to walk down the grassy bank onto the lane, he paused outside Steven Pearn's cottage. Maybe he should talk to the man after all and bring him into the coven. He knew Sandra would like that. He sighed; it was too risky. The man seemed to be on good terms with Doryty and that made him a danger to the cause. He decided against it and walked on, the man's forefathers may have lived in the village, but he grew up in a city where the old ways had failed to take root and the memory of the craft had withered and died. He would never understand.

# CHAPTER 19

It was a beautiful bright and sunny summer's morning which complimented the mood Steven was in. Shutting the gate behind him, he walked up the path to Doryty's front door and knocked lightly. Footsteps sounded from the lane, and Steven turned to see Andrew Trevan carrying a large bundle of kindling. Steven stared after him wondering, then Doryty opened the door and ushered him in.

'I thought the girl might be one of them,' Doryty said after listening to Steven's tale.

'Then why didn't you warn me?' he demanded, glaring at her, his nails biting into the arm of the chair.

'Not my way till there is some proof. You should know my ways by now.'

Steven calmed himself and apologised for the outburst. She was right, as usual. He knew Doryty would never blindly accuse anyone without proof; it just wasn't in her nature.

'Why did you suspect Sandra though?' he asked in a more reasonable tone.

'Cos she was in with my sister, saw them talking close more than once recently. I thought she might have been part of her coven. Marjory was all about passing things down to the next generation, you see, but she never told me no names,' Doryty smiled grimly. 'She liked to keep her little secrets from me.'

'Should I confront Sandra?' Steven said. 'Get her to tell me who the others are? Maybe I should call the police.'

Doryty looked worried by that suggestion. 'Don't see as the police can do anything but laugh at a foolish boy with nightmares and a witch paranoia,' she said.

Steven had to admit anyone with an ounce of sanity would have a hard time believing his story.

'And confronting her,' Doryty continued, 'will just make them go underground, anyway, like as not the girl will just deny it was her. You will have revealed your ace and gained nothing.'

He nodded at her wisdom, she was always right, and he was comforted to know that she was there with him in this.

'Try to play it cool, as the youngsters say these days,' she said. 'Tell her you have been to the bonfire site again and hint that you have found something revealing, but don't let her know you were there last night or that you know that she was a part of it. Look for her reactions; you will know if she is guilty. Check her phone too. Make a note of friends she has been texting recently, who she has arranged meetings with. I want to know who she is friends within the village too. When you find out bring it all to me. Together we will piece it all together.'

She gave Steven the usual squeeze of the hand, which always signalled the end of their discussion, and for once Steven left satisfied.

# CHAPTER 20

It was Saturday and both Steven and Sandra had the day off. Steven suggested they have a lazy day in the village. 'Maybe a meal at the pub? What do you say?' Steven asked as casually as he could. As he had hoped, Sandra said yes.

Their day was spent shopping locally and Steven found himself enjoying the day more than he had expected; although it had nothing to do with the company he was keeping. Despite his many trips to the West Coast he never tired of the quaint little village streets with shops full of trinkets and treats. He stood gazing at each shop window displaying their wares in a way that was sure to lure him in. It worked every time and Sandra shook her head and sighed as he came out laden with homemade sweets, or jams and chutneys or even a little ornament to keep company with the ones his nan had collected over the years, which he was yet to dispose of.

They were nearly at the pub where they had planned to have lunch when Steven spotted another old-fashioned sweet shop and quickly dived in before Sandra could stop him. Moments later he came out grinning as he shoved a piece of clotted cream whisky flavoured fudge into his mouth. He offered Sandra the bag, but she shook her head.

'The novelty does wear off eventually,' she said.

Steven nodded and made agreeable noises as he consumed more of the fudge, then quickly crossed the little lane to a shop that was selling a variety of different flavoured gins. 'But you don't even drink gin,' Sandra exclaimed dragging him away from the window.

*The Cursed Shore*

'But there is elderflower and orange,' he protested weakly.

'Let's just go to the pub and eat,' she said. 'It's past lunchtime and the summer chef Mike has working here this year is awesome.'

Steven made what he hoped was a cute little pouty face, but Sandra assured him he just looked like a constipated dog and continued to drag him away from the gin shop. With a sigh, he allowed himself to be led to the pub. He was supposed to be on a reconnaissance mission after all, and what better place to observe Sandra amongst her friends than the pub where she worked. Besides, he could come back to the Little Gin Emporium later. It was true that he didn't really like gin, but flavours like cherry rain and orange chocolate blitz simply had to be tried, and besides, the little jugs they were sold in were ceramic works of art in themselves. He paused for a moment as a worrying thought that he was turning into his nan drifted across his mind. A tug on his sleeve reminded him where he was supposed to be going and he dutifully trotted after Sandra as she disappeared into the Smugglers Rest.

The only concrete friendships Steven knew Sandra had, was her boss Mike the landlord of the Smugglers Rest, and Penny from the bank in town. Penny was Sandra's best friend, and she lived in the village too. He had already added Mike to the list of possible conspirators, but it was hard to place Penny there. She was so sweet and innocent, bordering on immature. He just couldn't picture her dressed up as a witch doing murderous rituals round a bonfire. Or maybe, like Sandra, that was the perfect cover for her.

As Steven and Sandra entered the pub, Mike came rushing out from behind the bar to welcome them, shaking Steven's hand vigorously. Steven smiled back; it was surprising how easy the acting came to him, no doubt it was the same for Sandra too.

Mike rushed off to get them the food and drinks they ordered, and Steven and Sandra went to sit by a back window with a view of the coastline. It had been a lovely morning. Steven reflected, maybe he could just forget all the bonfire stuff and thoughts of conspiracies and let himself enjoy the rest of the day. Then he thought of Doryty's disapproval and shivered. He looked around, half expecting to see her in a corner, glaring at him for having such thoughts. It was enough to pull him back on course and remember why he was here.

As Sandra sipped her drink, she answered a text on her phone.

'Do you mind if Penny pops by to say hello?' she said.

'Of course not,' Steven assured her, maybe a little too quickly.

He had already met Penny when he was registering his new address at the bank. She was sweet and bubbly, and he was sure she was flirting with him despite being Sandra's friend. He found he liked her a little more than he probably should. Luckily, Sandra did not seem to notice his enthusiasm and sent a text back to Penny.

Steven and Sandra had just finished eating when Penny came in, joining them with warm hugs and kisses, which Steven readily returned. Mike left the bar and joined them. Steven sat back in his chair and watched how the three interacted, trying to look beyond their light conversation and their smiles.

He wasn't sure what he should be looking for if he was honest. Of course, there was no mention of bonfires and rituals, why would there be? However, he was confused about how friendly they were towards him, it seemed so genuine. In the end he didn't even bother to study them, he just enjoyed the company and found himself laughing at the jokes like they were all good friends. There would be nothing sinister to report back to Doryty, not from this encounter, anyway.

*The Cursed Shore*

After they had said their goodbyes to Mike and Penny, they spent the afternoon lying on the beach and relaxing, before enjoying tea at a local café. The evening was to be spent at Steven's cottage with wine and a movie, lots of wine. Steven hoped to get Sandra drunk to afford him more chances to get a look at her phone. So far, he had avoided any intimacy between them, he may have enjoyed her company today and although she was attractive, attentive, and had amazing boobs, the thought of what she had been putting him through drove all the desire from him. Hopefully, she would be too drunk to notice this evening.

In the meantime, he dropped the occasional hint about the bonfire ritual.

'What if I went up there and confronted those people, asked what they were doing?' he said, casually stirring his spoon in his teacup and looking out of the window, admiring the view of the cliffs and the glittering azure sea beyond.

He was amazed at how calm Sandra was about this, and all the other mentions, of the ritual.

'Might be a good idea,' she said. 'Maybe you will find out that it's not quite what you think it is.' Then as he pondered on the thought that this might be an invitation, she added, 'Or maybe they will sacrifice you to their gods and your body will wash up on the morning tide.'

An invitation or a threat, maybe both. Sandra did not seem at all bothered by his comments and it irritated him immensely, but not enough to blurt out what he already knew. He gave himself a figurative pat on the back; he was getting better at being less emotional and more in control of himself.

Evening arrived at long last and Steven set the scene. Candles for a romantic evening he had told her. What he really wanted was a darkened room. A romantic film to add to the mood he had said as he chose a movie that he

*Ellen Hiller*

knew she would find boring and hoped she was too polite to say. He wanted her drunk and sleepy.

As he poured another glass of wine, her phone rang, and he jumped nervously. Luckily, she just giggled at him and answered it. It was Penny. Steven paused to listen in on the conversation. Apparently, Penny was going out tomorrow and they couldn't meet up. What a shame, he thought cynically, they won't be able to meet up and torture me. He wondered if that meant there wouldn't be a ritual tomorrow and he would be able to sleep without any bad experiences. Worth the risk, he thought, and he would dearly love to get a good night for once.

The film was suitably boring as he had hoped and with the day's long excursion, the warm evening, as well as two bottles of wine it did the trick. Sandra was lying against him gently snoring.

Her phone was in her handbag at the side of the sofa, and if he stretched his arm, he could just about reach in and get it. He moved slowly, not wanting to disturb her as his fingers brushed over the various miscellaneous items that filled it. Then he whispered a triumphant 'yes!' as his fingers finally curled around the phone's smooth edges. Praying silently that it wouldn't slip from his grasp, he gently lifted it out.

It was just a simple thing really, lying there with his girlfriend's phone in his hand, but he felt like a master criminal. He wouldn't have been surprised if there was a flash of blue lights outside the window and a sharp knock on the door. Nothing happened though, Sandra slept on and he typed her pass code, the one he had observed her using several times today, into the keypad.

Sandra's list of contacts seemed to be endless. How could one person know so many people? He only had about nine on his phone, and five of them he hadn't spoken to since he moved to Cornwall. He moved on to her text messages, this was more interesting.

*The Cursed Shore*

There were texts from Penny, of course. There were a few from Mike, her mum and about ten others that were recent and frequent. He looked at the messages themselves and things became a little more obvious. He had presumed the coven would use some kind of code, but no, the messages were brazen in their meaning. All was in plain sight. Nothing was hidden.

Arranging to meet up for the ritual almost every night were Sandra, Mike, someone called Alison, Peter Enys, the farmer who he had only just found out owned the land on which the bonfires took place, Penny, obviously not as innocent as she seemed, and Constable Andrew Trevan.

No surprise about Trevan, Steven thought, as he slid the phone back into her handbag. He gave Sandra a not so gentle nudge.

'Time to get you home, dear, you are quite worn out,' he said with a forced gentleness. He couldn't wait to get rid of her, she was a vile creature. How she must have laughed with her friends as she told them about his anguish and suffering. It was all he could do not to slap her awake and kick her out of the door. However, he was sensible enough to keep up the pretence.

He took her home, she was too drunk to even notice how icy he was to her, and then he headed back home for some sleep. Luckily there was some wine left over, he would need something to calm him down before he headed off to bed.

# CHAPTER 21

'Mike the landlord? Well I never.' Doryty had eaten up the new information with enthusiasm, pulling out a notebook of her own to jot down the details along with some dots and squiggles he presumed must be a form of shorthand.

'Not surprised about Peter Enys though, he owns the land atop the cliff path.'

'Yeah, I worked that one out too,' Steven said.

'Aye lad, it's no wonder he is part of it.'

'It seems as though the whole village is conspiring against me,' Steven said as he slumped back into his chair. Doryty reached over and gave his hand the usual reassuring squeeze.

'Except you, Doryty, I would be lost if it wasn't for you.' Doryty nodded in agreement, modesty wasn't her style.

'Then I think it's high time you bought an old lady a drink, don't you?' she said.

'Err sure,' Steven agreed, surprised by this new turn of events. Usually this was tea and cake time.

'What are you planning, Doryty?' he asked.

'Just want Mike to see me and you together, is all. To see his reaction. I think it's time they all knew we were on to them, don't you?' Steven breathed out a long and heavy sigh. Yes, he did think it was about time something was done. He was sick of playing victim in their cruel games.

Doryty bustled about finding a suitable coat and hat, despite the warm weather, then disappeared upstairs to 'fetch a clean hanky.' It was just the sort of thing his own grandmother would have said, and he basked in the warmth of feeling part of a family once more.

By midday, Steven and Doryty were sitting in the Smugglers Rest watching Mike the landlord holding court over his regulars and tourists alike. The pub was a low whitewashed building with a slate roof that somehow sagged in the middle yet had never fallen in. Steven didn't know how old it was, but it looked ancient. The style of pub endeared it to tourists as well as the regulars, and it was always full to capacity with a lively atmosphere and good company. Inside there were comfortable chairs, wooden beams and a gigantic stone hearth that would contain a roaring log fire on a winter's evening. A perfect Cornish pub. He loved it and it was here that he had first met Sandra. He forced those once happy memories from his mind as he brought the drinks over to a little table Doryty had picked out. It gave them a full view of the bar and vice versa.

Mike, however, apart from a brisk hello, paid them no attention as he handed out drinks to his customers across the polished oak bar, with a cheery smile and a joke and tried to impress the barmaid with his peanut catching skills.

'He wants to be careful,' Doryty said as she sipped her sherry. Mike threw another peanut into the air. 'Easy to choke on one of those,' she added.

The instant Doryty said these words, Mike, who had expertly caught the nut in his mouth, made a gasping sound and clutched hold of the bar with one hand, madly gesturing to his throat with the other.

'Yeah, very funny Mike,' came a voice from the back of the bar and the barmaid laughed nervously.

Another more concerned voice answered, 'I think he really is choking.'

*Ellen Hiller*

By now, Mike was clearly in distress and his red face was beginning to take on a purple hue. The barmaid started frantically patting him on the back, but it wasn't working.

Steven jumped up from his chair to help but Doryty grabbed his jacket and pulled him down again. 'Let's just see how this plays out,' she said.

Steven was shocked, he went to stand again, but was relieved to see others had already rushed to Mike's aid. There was now a small crowd around him, some banging his back and others shouting advice. Someone shouted to use the Heimlich manoeuvre, and another answered that they thought they knew how to do it.

Mike was now slumped over the bar, he looked unconscious, no longer fighting to breathe. A large man tried the manoeuvre, but Mike just slipped to the floor.

'I think he's dead,' someone shouted, and an ambulance siren could be heard in the distance.

'Time to go, dearie,' Doryty said as she stood and buttoned up her coat and adjusted her hat. 'We're just in the way here.'

Steven followed her out of the bar like a small child being led away from a schoolyard fight by his granny. He kept looking over his shoulder to see what was happening but Doryty's firm hand on his back pushed him along and kept him moving out and away from the gathering crowd.

'Come on now, dear,' she kept saying, 'this way now.' Like a child Steven let himself be led. He wasn't sure if it was fatigue but once more the world around him was beginning to feel unreal again. He had become a spectator of his own life and all he could do was look on and try to keep up with the plot.

'But we were there to watch him, to confront him about the bonfire ritual, and now he could be dead,' he heard himself saying.

'Funny old world, isn't it, dear.' Doryty didn't even try to sound reassuring, she just kept guiding him along through the village until somehow, they were outside his

*The Cursed Shore*

cottage door. He fumbled in his pockets for his keys as he rested his forehead against the cool wooden door. Then, when he finally got the key in the lock, he turned to say something to Doryty. However, she was nowhere to be seen.

Steven went inside and sank down into the sofa, head in hands, and feeling lost and alone. He shuddered; this was his life now he thought, snatches of sleep, mystic cliff rituals and strange deaths along with the horrific nightmares. Somehow, he was in the middle of something surreal with no idea how he got there, except a distant connection to one of the original murdered smugglers.

He closed his eyes and prayed for a peaceful dreamless sleep, so he didn't have to think about his life any longer.

# CHAPTER 22

Penny loved to shop and when the mood took her, Truro was her favourite destination. Here she could find all the big-name stores, as well as a good cluster of unique boutiques. The perfect place to find everything she needed for her upcoming holiday to Spain, and she intended to make a full day of it.

She did feel a little guilty about not being able to get back in time for tonight's ritual, but she knew after a hard day shopping, she would need a good night's sleep before work tomorrow. Anyway, it wasn't as if she would be missed. She was sure that she was only there to make up the numbers. Her aunty may have been a witch, but she was sure that not a single strand of the craft ran through her own DNA. It did make her feel special though, standing on the clifftop in front of the roaring flames. When she was there, she was a part of something exotic and ancient. As soon as she put on her robe, she was different somehow, more serious, grown up, responsible.

Then Marjory died, and the bodies started to wash up on the shore and she realised that this was more than just a dramatic cosplay. This was real and frightening and what they were doing clearly was no longer working. When Marjory was here, she gloried in being part of the coven that kept Aglets safe. Now it all seemed pointless.

At least today, she had an excuse not to attend, and she wouldn't have to look Andrew in the eye when he wondered why it didn't work. She was sure it was all her fault.

*The Cursed Shore*

At last, it was time to leave the busy streets of Truro and Penny bundled her bags full of wondrous retail therapy onto the back seat of her ancient little Mini before she headed home. Soon she was cruising through the leafy lanes again, the car window was open, and the evening breeze was blowing in. Time for music, she thought and turned on the radio.

Penny had taken her eyes off the road for mere seconds to switch radio stations, and when she looked up again, she was shocked to see someone in front of her, an old woman just standing there in the middle of the road. Her brain didn't have time to process the information, her body acted on impulse as she slammed on the breaks and swerved to avoid the woman. She swerved too wide, her wheel hit the edge of the ditch at the side of the road and she screamed as she lost control of the steering wheel. The breaks were not responding. In fact, the car seemed to be going faster than ever, straight towards a huge elm tree.

The world slowed down; she knew she would hit the tree. She had time to think of her mother and wondered if she would be able to cope on her own. She thought about work and how much her sudden death would be an inconvenience to her boss. She thought of the coven and hoped her presence at the nightly rituals would not be missed. She even had time to regret not fastening her seatbelt before driving out of the car park such a short time ago. Then there was no more time to think. The tree filled her vision, then there was the sound of metal crunching violently and she had the sensation of flying before the world came to an abrupt stop and everything went dark.

Doryty studied the wreck of the car and sensing no life from the crumpled and bleeding girl, tutted and shook her head, then shuffled off down the lane towards the bus stop.

# CHAPTER 23

Peter Enys was up early to make a start on the potato harvest. A low-lying mist covered the farm and made it eerily quiet, but the sun was rising quickly, and he knew from experience it would soon burn the mist off and replace it with a hot sunny day.

He had two small fields to do today and due to the way business had been going lately, he couldn't afford to pay for extra labour. It was going to be long and exhausting day.

Still, no sense brooding about it, he thought as he walked over to the harvester and started her up.

Three hours into his work, Peter decided it was time for a tea break when a sudden jolt brought the harvester to an abrupt halt. Cursing under his breath, he switched the engine off and climbed out of the cab. He already knew what the problem would be; there would be a lump of rock, usually granite, stuck in the rollers somewhere. The field had been ploughed so many times over the years you would have thought every rock and stone had already been unearthed, but no, there was always at least one, lying in wait, ready to jam up the works and make his day that much harder.

Peter unhooked the metal bar from the side of the cab that was there for the very purpose of prising out stubborn stones and walked around the side of the harvester to check the rollers.

'Ah shit!' Peter said, seeing a very large lump of rock was right at the top of the rollers. As if this wasn't going to

*The Cursed Shore*

slow him up already, he now had to climb up on the machinery to get at it.

Once at the top Peter wasted no time and set to work with the bar trying to pop the stone out. He managed to get some leverage by pushing all his weight on the rubber covering the steel rollers. There was a little movement, so he pushed down harder on the bar. As he did so, he lost his grip on the bar and it slipped out of his hands, clattering through the rollers before hitting the earth with a soul-destroying thud.

Peter screamed his bad luck to the heavens and took his temper out on the rock, kicking it with his boot and stamping on it to try to push it through the rollers. One huge stamp and as his foot hit the rock, he looked up to see old Miss Doryty standing there, next to the harvester, watching him. He jumped back in surprise and nearly lost his balance. What on earth was the horrid woman doing here? She had no business being on his farm and she knew it. She may have been Marjory's sister, but that didn't mean she had any business with him. He didn't want her here on his land that was for sure.

Doryty smiled up at Peter as if unaware of his feelings towards her. She reached down to pick up the metal bar and benevolently handed it up to him. He had to bend over and stretch his arm out to reach it, but he was grateful for her help. Maybe he had misjudged the woman. At that moment, the harvester engines spluttered back to life, the rock crumbled, and the rollers started to turn. It all happened in seconds.

Peter yelped more in shock than pain as his foot caught in the roller. 'Doryty! Quick, turn the engine off!' he yelled over the noise of the machinery, whilst fighting to free his trapped foot. But the rollers kept turning, unrelenting, pulling his foot further in and crushing his ankle bones with a loud crunch. Now he screamed in pain as it overrode the shock. 'Doryty! Turn it off!' he yelled.

Doryty didn't turn the harvester off. She simply stood there watching as inch by inch Peter's leg was pulled into the machinery.

Screaming and flailing about Peter lost his balance, his free leg slipping into the rollers too. His screaming reached an even higher pitch, and still the rollers kept on going, unrelentingly pulling him further into the machine. He tried to grab at the sides of the harvester, tried to find something solid to hold on to, if he could not pull himself out, he might at least be able to stop himself from being pulled in. but his hands could find no purchase on the smooth metal and he cried out in frustration.

The pain was making it hard for Peter to breathe. He was dizzy and nauseous and with every inch of him that was pulled into the machine there came that same blood-curdling crunching sound of his bones being pulverised.

Both legs were gone now, he could not feel the bloody pulp they had become, and it was fortunate that he could not see it. When he thought the pain could not get any worse, the rollers found a new place to crush, and it reached a new intensity. They had reached his groin now, and he howled like a dying animal as they moved unrelenting up his torso. Here there was more to crush than bones, his screams took on a gurgling sound as the mulch that had been his organs, and intestines were pushed upwards.

That was when the screaming abruptly stopped. Unfortunately, for Peter it was not because he was dead but that the bloody mulch was filling his lungs and choking him, there was no air left to scream with, and still the rollers kept pulling him in.

Pain was all he had now. There was no hope of rescue and Peter knew that he would be dead soon. The last thing he saw as his vision faded was Doryty slowly walking away in the direction of the cliff path.

# CHAPTER 24

Steven awoke and stretched; sleep had left him refreshed for the first time in what seemed like years. For the first few blissful moments his mind was blank, it could have been any summer's morning on any day of his life, as he lay there listening to the sound of the sea. He loved the boom of the large waves far out to sea coupled with the gentle slosh of the smaller ones as they flowed gently into the cove. As he listened to the soothing sounds he was gently lulled back to sleep.

A seagull screeched loudly outside his bedroom window making him jump. Now fully awake, the memories of the previous day started to creep, unbidden, into his mind and he groaned and looked at his watch. It was 9 a.m. Steven had slept all yesterday afternoon and a whole night too. No nightmares, not even a dream to spoil it. Despite the previous day's events, he forced himself to enjoy the moment and went down to the kitchen to make breakfast. He couldn't remember the last time he had eaten more than a snack, or for that matter, the last time he was hungry.

After a lengthy breakfast, he decided to pop in and see Doryty. How soon, he thought, had this strange old lady become his friend and confidant.

Doryty, however, was not at home. Steven wandered around the village looking for her. She always seemed to be at home, especially when he needed her, but today she was nowhere to be seen. Eventually he gave up looking and went back to get his car. He had written a piece about Mike's death for the *Recorder* and thought he would hand it in himself rather than email it. Show John how sober and on top of things he was today.

Typically, John had been extremely pleased that Steven had been in the pub that lunchtime and witnessed the whole event. It added to the authenticity to the article he had said, and Steven said he was glad to have obliged and left for home, citing another headache.

Once he had returned, via Doryty's house, who still was not at home, Steven was wondering if he should have another nap on the sofa, just to see if his luck would hold out. However, as he sat down and started to make himself comfortable, his phone rang. It was Sandra. A pang of guilt washed over him. How soon he had forgotten her. As far as she knew he was still her boyfriend, yet he hadn't been in touch for a couple of days.

Sandra was sobbing as he answered the call. No surprise there, Mike had been her boss, not to mention her friend, it seemed. Steven started to give his condolences and pretended to care, saying what a terrible accident it was, that he had always known that they were good friends, and how he would be missed.

Through Sandra's sobs, she managed to choke out 'no, not Mike, yes that was horrible too, but it's Penny this time, my friend Penny, she was killed this morning.' Steven was completely taken aback and could not find the words to answer so Sandra carried on. 'It was a freak accident while she was driving back from Truro, apparently. Witnesses say she swerved to avoid something, although they could not see what, and the car went down an embankment, and hit a tree.'

Sandra began sobbing again, and Steven tried to find some soothing words, but he was still at a total loss. 'Knowing Penny, it was probably some little critter in the road that she didn't want to hit,' he said. Sandra broke into fresh sobs as she agreed with him.

He gave Sandra his condolences once more and asked if she needed company this evening. He was relieved when

*The Cursed Shore*

she said that she needed to be alone, a bullet he was happy to dodge. Then as there was nothing else to do, he set out to try Doryty's house one more time.

This time when he knocked, he heard the familiar shuffling before the door opened slowly.

'Doryty! At last, I've something I must tell you. Where have you been all day?'

The old woman gave him her sweetest smile and answered. 'Oh, I just popped into Truro to do some shopping, dearie, nothing to worry yourself over, would you like to come in for some tea?'

Steven forgot to breathe for a moment then politely declined the invitation, turned on his heel and headed back home. His head was beginning to fill with the familiar fog of disbelief that had blighted his life for the last month. He needed to get away from Doryty for a while and try to think this through himself. His hand shook so much he could hardly get the key in the lock of the cottage door. He was cold and trembling so once inside he lit the fire and made coffee, trying to keep his body busy as he fought to control of his mind.

Penny and Mike, two of the bonfire conspirators he had told Doryty about, both dead in short succession. How much did you have to stretch your imagination to believe it was just a tragic coincidence? Added to that, Doryty had been in the pub and Doryty had been in Truro.

Steven sat on his sofa with his cooling coffee mug in his hands. His hands were trembling so much he could not get the thing to his lips. Eventually he gave up and set it back on the table.

Was it his fault? he wondered. He had, after all, given the names to Doryty and now they were dead. Even though they had been his tormentors, his enemies, did that deserve a death sentence? Then there was Sandra. True, he no longer harboured any romantic feelings for her, but he did not wish her dead either.

In thinking this way, however, he was suggesting that a little old lady who cared for him like a grandmother and who loved her afternoon tea and cake, had murdered two people merely because he had told her they were hurting him. That was taking the protective grandmother persona too far. None of this made any sense. Nothing ever did these days.

Once more Steven sat with his head in his hands, utterly overwhelmed with disbelief, he felt he was drowning all over again. 'Why is all this happening?' was becoming his new catchphrase.

Tomorrow he would have to confront Doryty again and this time he would not let her evade his questions. No more half answers that were meaningless. A confusion of emotions; he was angry with her, but thankful she was on his side at the same time. He wondered if there was anything he could or should have done differently, but the thoughts and ideas just ran circles through his head, and he had to force himself to stop.

There would be no sleep tonight, even though he was sure that there would be no one on that clifftop lighting bonfires. He thought of Sandra alone and grieving for her friends and regretted not confronting her before telling Doryty what he knew. Would it have made a difference he wondered? Why had he been letting Doryty make all his decisions for him?

Steven brooded on the events all evening and into the night. He paced the floor now, kicking at the furniture and growling under his breath. No, this would not wait until morning he finally decided. He needed answers now. Not caring about the time, Steven left the cottage, letting the door slam behind him and set out for Doryty's once more.

Steven was aware that banging on an old lady's front door in the middle of the night was likely to draw attention, but he no longer cared. He needed Doryty to wake up and to hear what he had to say.

*The Cursed Shore*

Andrew Trevan lived just down the lane, and Steven wondered if he would come to Doryty's aid when he heard all the banging. That would make things more interesting, he thought. Steven knocked even louder, hoping the constable would hear.

Eventually, he heard shuffling behind the door and the metallic chink of bolts sliding back and the door swung open, revealing a furious Doryty.

'Huh! Doesn't like her sleep disturbed either,' he thought as he waited to be scolded like a naughty boy. Instead, once the old woman saw who it was, she smiled kindly at him and gently patted his back as she ushered Steven in.

Once he was sat in his usual comfy chair, with the cat in place on his lap, Steven immediately felt ashamed of himself for being angry at her. She was only trying to help him after all. She was always helping him, and he had no right to be angry with her. He looked about the room and wondered what it was that soothed him. Why was he so compliant when he was here? He tried to be angry again, to tap back into the rage he felt before, but there was no heat to it, just a creeping despair.

'I can't take it anymore, Doryty,' Steven cried. 'I've passed snapping point, I'm not even sure if I'm still sane. One day I am living a normal life in the city, the next I'm living in a small coastal village and surrounded by death and conspiracy. Random dead people haunting me in my waking hours, and I die in my sleeping ones. Is it all my fault? I never asked for any of it. I love Cornwall, but why did everything in my life turn into a horror story when I moved here? It has to stop, Doryty, I can't take it anymore.'

'If you have reached this point, then it must be time,' Doryty stated solemnly.

Steven looked up to meet the eyes of the old lady.

'What do you mean?'

'You must kill Andrew Trevan. Tea, dearie?'

# CHAPTER 25

Andrew Trevan's hand trembled slightly as he lifted the glass to his lips. Mike was dead. That fact would never change, no matter how he felt about it. The world would continue today, and the world would continue tomorrow, just as it always had, just as it would always would. But his best friend would no longer be a part of it. The brandy burnt his throat as he gulped it down, his second glass. How many more before the pain dulled, he wondered.

Andrew and Mike had been friends since the day they were sat next to each other on the first day of primary school. He knew, had known, the man better than his own family. Now there was just a yawning chasm in his life, and he knew nothing would ever fill it.

A peanut, for Christ's sake. A peanut! Something so small and insignificant and it wiped out the future of a man and everything he could have experienced in life. It was so unfair, unjust, and unlikely. How on earth was he supposed to come to terms with it?

Andrew wiped his eyes and forced himself to stop trying to find reason where there would never be any. Better to remember his friend in happy times, he told himself without believing it.

His mobile phone buzzed, he glanced at it not intending to answer it until he saw Sandra's name on the caller ID. Mike had been her friend too; they had even dated for a few months. He guessed there was company in grief and answered the call.

'Hey Sandra, how are you coping?' he asked.

*The Cursed Shore*

'I'm not, not at all,' she all but squeaked back at him and he pictured her trying to hold back the sobs as she spoke.

'We've lost Penny too.'

Andrew was too stunned to reply with more than a grunt. 'Huh?'

'I just got a call from her mum, she's distraught. Penny died in a freak car accident this morning … Andrew? Are you still there?'

Andrew was dumbstruck. Penny dead too, this sort of thing just didn't happen.

'How can this be a coincidence?' he croaked, his voice breaking up as he pushed the words out. 'Do you think it could be Doryty?'

'I thought the same,' said Sandra. 'But how is she suddenly so powerful? I'm scared Steven might be involved in some way. He has this crazy connection to the past which makes me think he might have something of the craft in him, and he seems to think the old hag is his friend. Do you think it could be him? Please say no.'

Andrew paused, deep in thought.

'Even if they are working together, how do we prove it, Sandra?' he finally said. 'And more importantly, how do we stop it?'

Now there was a direction to point it, Andrew's grief turned quickly to anger.

'I want to go down there and strangle the bitch, maybe that will stop her. Is there anything in Marjory's book that will see her off without leaving any evidence?' he asked.

'No there won't be, the craft isn't for using like that, you know that just as well as I do, Andrew,' Sandra said.

'Someone should tell that to Doryty then. We are in danger, Sandra. If she knows about Mike and Penny, she likely knows about the rest of us too. How on earth did she find out?' he asked.

'Well she knew you and I were friends with Marjory, not a huge leap to know we were a part of her coven.

Maybe she has been planning this since Marjory died, maybe before even.'

Andrew nodded, then realising she couldn't see him said, 'Yeah, we need to watch our backs. I will get word out to the others; Peter should know first...' He paused then went on, 'He should have phoned me this morning; he hasn't been in touch. You don't think...'

'Don't even think it,' Sandra cried. 'He could be caught up doing anything, probably working and forgot to call. Please let it be that.'

Andrew had a sick feeling in his stomach that maybe it was more, but he clung to the thought that he was probably being paranoid.

'Right,' he said, 'I don't care what you say this time, Sandra, I'm making charm pouches for you and the others. I know you think they are gross but, well, at least it's something, you know?' He reached for his own charm pouch, hanging from the cord around his neck, and felt the comforting tingle of its protection.

'Yeah,' she agreed, 'thanks, Andrew. I will feel better wearing one now.'

'Come early to the ritual tonight,' he said. 'I will make sure the others do too, we have a lot to discuss.'

'What if this scares the others off, Andrew? What if we don't have enough to do the ritual anymore?'

'Chance we have to take, I guess. Who knows, it might even inspire them to work harder, I'm sure some of them don't take it seriously enough. We need to come up with a group plan to get rid of Doryty too, once and for all.'

'Andrew, do you think she had anything to do with Marjory's death?' Sandra asked, a noticeable quiver in her voice. 'She must have always known that she needed her out of the way before the curse could be let loose again.'

'I have no idea, Sandra,' he answered. 'Let's just agree that she is capable of anything and take it from there.'

Sandra agreed and hung up. The room was silent again, oppressively so. The grief that his anger had pushed aside for the moment crept back in from the darkened corners of the room and smothered him. He poured himself another drink.

# CHAPTER 26

'It was my sister's fault, always interfering, poking her nose in where it wasn't welcome,' Doryty explained as she poured the tea. 'No respect for the old ways, the ancient ways. Interfering old bitch is what she was. Should not have had to come to this. It's not your fault, dearie, it's hers.'

These were not the words Steven had expected to hear. Hearing the word 'bitch' coming from the mouth of such a sweet old lady made it seem even more offensive and he couldn't help but cringe when she said it. Moreover, what exactly had Marjory been interfering with, he wondered. He shifted uneasily in his chair. The once cosy room was slowly becoming cold and unwelcoming. Even the cat jumped from his lap and ran from the room. If Doryty noticed, she didn't let it bother her as she ranted on, the bitterness dripping through her words.

Steven interrupted Doryty to voice something he was finding hard to understand.

'So, you are saying Sandra and her friends were trying to stop the curse?'

'Stop it? No one can stop it,' Doryty replied with obvious frustration. 'A witch's death curse does not end, never ends. You can slow it down, pause it even, build a wall around it and hope it never gets out, if you want, but it can never be stopped. Nor should it be. A Scadden witch, my kin, died a torturous death for nowt more than a few shillings to buy a little comfort from the cold nights. There should be no comfort for those that killed her.'

*The Cursed Shore*

'But that was well over two hundred years ago,' Steven shot back. 'Those who killed her are long dead and buried. The people dying now are innocent victims; they know nothing of your ancestor's fate. They can't be held to blame. I doubt they even know anything about their own ancestors, and what they did back then. They do not deserve this, Doryty!'

'They don't deserve it. That's what your head's telling you, aint it? But what's your heart telling you, boy? How does it feel to know a Trevan still lives in Aglets Cove?'

Steven gripped the arms of the chair, unable to stop the sudden surge of rage that exploded in him at the mention of Trevan's name. He choked back the taste of cold seawater in his throat, and the panic that followed. Hugging himself against the sudden chill of the room, Steven let his lips ask the question that his brain was trying to pretend he wasn't asking.

'So, will killing a Trevan end my nightmares once and for all? And why him? What about the others?'

Old Miss Doryty sat back in her chair and calmly sipped her tea, her eyes gleaming at him over the rim of her cup. Quietly, she murmured, 'A Trevan has yet to die. Kin of all the others, that's long been sorted, over and over in some cases; but never a Trevan, and he was the worst of the lot.'

Steven tried to think his way out of what was implied. A smart sane answer like 'no I'm not committing murder to fulfil a centuries old curse,' but all that came out was 'Why does it have to be me? It's hardly fair.'

He knew his plea was childlike but once more, that was exactly how he felt. A child with no control over his life, being told what to do for his own good by the grown-ups.

'Why you?' Doryty screeched the words at him causing him to lurch back into his chair, seeking protection from its overstuffed cushions. He hadn't seen this side of old Miss Doryty before, what had happened to the sweet little old lady that he knew? He wanted her back. He needed

*Ellen Hiller*

her, and he knew that he had to do whatever she wanted to get the grandmother he needed her to be, back again.

'Why you? Why my ancestor? Why yours? They didn't ask for what happened to them, but they passed the baton on as it were, to their kin, to us, to honour their memory and avenge their murder.'

Doryty lowered her voice again, once more assuming the guise of a kindly old lady, but her words were just as chilling.

'I'm surprised you never asked why the murders started again after so long a break,' she said. 'Not much of an investigative reporter, are you, dear?'

'So, tell me then,' Steven mumbled not quite sure he wanted to hear the answer.

Doryty squealed in delight, she had clearly been waiting for this moment.

'You should have been asking why they stopped in the first place.'

Steven shifted uneasily in his chair. He hadn't thought of that.

'You see, dear,' Doryty continued, 'after the first flourish of Revenue men's deaths all those years ago, it took some powerful witchcraft to keep the curse at bay. That witchcraft came from the traitors of Sarah Scadden's coven, she who had set the curse in motion. They betrayed her and her craft. "Do no harm," they said, "to protect the village from her evil," they promised. So, they worked together over the years to subdue the curse. They found a way to create a mirrored wall as it were, that was powerful enough to reflect the curse back to her who had sent it. Then to make sure the protection remained in place they passed the mantle on to future generations of the coven when they themselves became too old to carry on.' Doryty took a step closer to Steven and leaned over to hiss in his ear, 'Till the last of them powerful enough to do the ritual died last month.'

*The Cursed Shore*

'Your sister, of course.' Steven said, the whole enormity of what he had missed slowly sinking in.

'Aye, my sister and her stinking cat. Glad to see the back of them, I was.'

Steven immediately looked for his little furry nemesis, but it was nowhere to be seen. It had always been there watching him, now it wasn't in its usual spot he found he missed its comforting purrs.

'My sister and my ma before her, and so on, back through the family, all trying to stop the curse. For the sake of the village, they said. "Twernt right what was done," they said. Couldn't stop it though, could they? They stalled it, slowed it down some, put that wall up, but no, they never could have ended it. They expected me to join them too, and those that came after me, But I'm the last Scadden witch and I haven't a mind to stall it let alone end it.'

'Why haven't you killed a Trevan before now then?' Steven forced the words from his parched throat, fearing the wrath of the old lady once more.

Doryty sat back into the chair with her arms crossed, almost hugging herself. There was no sign of the fierce old witch that had been there previously. Now she looked even more frail and vulnerable and Steven was ashamed for having asked the question and desperately wanted to help her.

'Would if I could, boy, would if I could. Andrew Trevan will not be beguiled into anything by me, especially as he knows the old ways almost as well as I do. He's a cunning man that one. I am tired, dearie. How can an old lady like me stand up against the likes of him? However, you, my dear, you are young and strong, and you have a strong connection to your kinsman Jacob Pearn. The nightmares are proof of that connection. They are telling you what was suffered. Their spirits want you to end it; Jacob wants you to end it.'

Steven nodded, he knew that Jacob Pearn had been reaching out to him all this time, and he knew that Doryty would win any argument. He knew it was down to him alone to get the job done. The nightmares had proved he was the chosen one. The man to execute a Trevan. It was always so obvious when he spoke to Doryty.

'Will this save Sandra?' he asked. Up to now, he had avoided mentioning Doryty's obvious involvement in the recent deaths. He hoped she understood what was being asked.

'Silly girl might think twice before playing at witching after this,' Doryty said.

Steven knew he would get nothing more than that out of Doryty and he did not want to anger her by pressing the point. He still wasn't sure if Sandra and her friends were the good guys or the bad guys. The fact that they were involved in all this and not one of them, especially Sandra, thought to share what they were doing with him was enough to think them bad for the moment, but he did not want to think too hard about it.

Besides, whenever he tried to reason something out, his head just became muzzy and his brain refused to work. It was much easier when he just accepted Doryty's word and got on with it.

Steven left the cottage in a dreamlike state. Nothing seemed real anymore. Nothing, except for Doryty's final words: 'I have almost removed all the Trevan family's protection spells, taken best part of my life, but I got them all but one. Something physical still remains. No doubt, it's because he is wearing a charm or amulet of some sort. He does not trust me so it's no use me looking for it, but you could get close enough to find it and remove it. Do it at the beach and then let the spell do its work. Don't worry, it won't be you killing him, it will be his forefathers' victims that will see to that. His blood for their blood.'

*The Cursed Shore*

Steven knew what she meant; it was so obvious the way she told it. Innocent or not, the bloodline had a price to pay, just as he was paying it, night after night, freezing cold, drowned by rain and sea in his nightmares. At last, he had the power to end the nightmares and the visions that were haunting him. He was fated to put an end to all this, and he had to do it now, before he had time to question himself. Do what Doryty asked and everything would return to normal once more and he could forget about witches, curses, murders, and nightmares.

Steven stood on the street with his mobile phone in his hand, chilled to the bone despite the warm summer evening, and keyed in Trevan's personal number.

His stomach churned as Trevan answered the phone. He was sure Trevan would instantly know he was being spun a web of lies and Steven's cliché words sounded corny and unreal as they left his lips.

'I've found something on the beach,' Steven said. 'I think it's to do with the recent deaths, it will prove they were murders and not accidents after all... No, I don't want to call the station, I don't want to look stupid if I'm wrong. Be a mate and meet me down there will you? It might not be anything, but if it is, I don't want the tide to wash away something that might be important.'

Steven waited trembling for the answer. Please don't ask what it is, he prayed silently. Then Trevan's slightly confused voice came back.

'Sure, no problem, I can be there in ten minutes.'

# CHAPTER 27

Andrew Trevan slid the phone back into his pocket and reached down to put on his shoes. What could Steven possibly have found on the beach, and what was he doing down there at this time of night anyway? he wondered. He knew it wouldn't be another body, not this time but judging by how nervous Steven sounded maybe he really had found something. Whatever it was, Andrew was sure of one thing, Doryty would be involved somehow.

He paced around the small living room, what did the reporter hope to gain by talking to him personally, he thought he had made it quite clear after their last encounter that he wasn't someone that wanted to talk off the record. Maybe he was over thinking it though, there was nothing to say Steven hadn't found something sinister-looking on the beach and wanted his opinion. He wanted it to be this, he really did. But, if the reporter was making connections between the death of his friends and the bodies washed up on the beach, there would be some awkward questions to evade.

Andrew sighed and picked up his car keys, then hesitated and put them down again. He'd had far too much to drink, and besides, it might not pay to advertise where he was if things ended badly.

He decided to walk to the beach, taking the shortcut that passed Steven's cottage. After putting him to all this trouble it had better be something good, he thought, swaying slightly as he walked to the door. He really should not have drunk so much brandy, he thought, he hated not

*The Cursed Shore*

being totally in control of his body. At least he was comfortably numb now.

As the front door closed behind him, Andrew reached up and touched the hag stone that hung from the porch. Instantly, its calming power ran through him, and some of the mounting tension left his body. Finally, as was his ritual whenever he left the house, he checked the charm pouch he wore around his neck was safely in place, tucking it discreetly out of sight under his shirt. Then he walked down his garden path between the avenue of witches bottles. Can't be too careful he thought and grinned at the thought of Doryty watching him as he strode confidently past her window.

Thinking of Doryty, however, brought back the pain he had been trying to hold back. He clenched his fists, his nails biting deep into the palms of his hands. Mike and Penny gone, and they still hadn't heard from Peter.

There was nothing he could have done to stop it, he tried to tell himself, except maybe kill the old hag after Marjory had died. He knew it was her, he couldn't prove anything of course, but it was her alright. The thought that she could not touch him made him feel even more guilty about the others dying.

Why hadn't they done more to protect themselves as he had told them to do? He surmised that not being a descendant of a Revenue man gave them a false sense of security. Now there was only a few villagers left that knew about the old ways and he was afraid it wouldn't be enough to work with.

He patted his pocket and thought of Sandra, the charm pouch he had made for her was still safely there. He would take it over to her tonight and make sure she wore it. He hoped his magic was as good as his grandmas was when she had made his, and then at least Sandra would be safe while he worked on the others.

Why had Marjory not seen this coming and better prepared them for it, he wondered. She always wanted to see the best in her sister, always expected her to come over to their side. Despite their differences, there was a strong family bond between them. He wondered if Marjory kept Doryty at bay or if Doryty simply waited until Marjory was gone before she acted.

Soon he was standing at the top of the stone steps that took you down to the beach. The fact that they were the same steps that his ancestor had walked down all those years ago was not lost on him. A curse of his own, his murderous craven ancestor and an unfair guilt Andrew carried on his shoulders because of him. A guilt that Marjory had capitalised on when she introduced him to her coven. He smiled at the memory, she had given him a way to fight back against his heritage and hopefully absolve his family's name. Well that had been the plan anyway.

From where he stood, Andrew could see Steven Pearn pacing backwards and forwards at the water's edge, clearly agitated about something. He untucked the pouch from his shirt and held it for a moment, letting its power give him the confidence he needed to deal with whatever the reporter was about to throw at him, then he carefully walked down the worn and aged steps and pretended he couldn't see the ghosts of the past as they flittered past him.

# CHAPTER 28

Pushing aside a wave of nausea, Steven waved and walked over to Andrew Trevan as he entered the sandy cove via the stone steps, and he gestured towards the shoreline. When at last they were walking side-by-side Steven mumbled something about manacles and a chain. A worried look flitted across the constable's face, but his jolly demeanour remained as he chatted about the warm evening and maybe having drunk too much brandy.

As Trevan babbled on, the words were nothing more than indistinct noises to Steven's ears; his only focus was what had to be the amulet hanging from a leather cord around the man's neck. It was a small leather pouch tied tightly and bulging with things Steven could only imagine. Just like the hag stone that hung above his door and the witches bottles in the garden, the Trevan's had found a way to protect themselves through the generations. Using witchcraft against the witch.

Steven muttered affirmations to Taverns statements without really listening to what was being said. That small charm had all his attention and he could feel his heart thumping wildly at the excitement of being so close to it. All he had to do was snatch the pouch away from Trevan and the dead would claim their final victim. A Trevan would die and, the debt paid, the nightmares would end.

The thought of regaining his sanity and going back to a normal life again was all the reason Steven needed right now. Taking an amulet from a man wasn't really murder, was it? he reasoned with himself. But whether he believed it or not, there was no going back now. More than thought

*Ellen Hiller*

or reason he was experiencing a compulsion he had no resistance to, it was if someone else inhabited his body, forcing him to follow its commands. There was no room for any other thought in his mind now, only the amulet. He had to take it.

They reached the water's edge and Steven shivered as if a fever had swept over him and sweat beaded on his forehead. Dark clouds came from nowhere to cover the moon and a chill wind started to blow. His breath was shallow and fast as he knew the moment was approaching and a familiar anger began stirring through his body as he looked at the man.

Trevan had stopped talking and was looking at Steven oddly. There was no more time to waste. The moment had come. Steven lashed out and made a grab for the pouch with one hand, whilst fending off the shocked police officer with the other. A shrill, girl-like giggle came from the edge of the cove causing both men to look up simultaneously.

A deep circle had been carved into the sand encompassing the area under the old rusty mooring ring, and in that circle stood Doryty.

'I should have known!' roared Trevan across the beach to her. 'Come to watch your dirty work done for you, hag?'

Whilst keeping a firm grip on the young constable and the other hand still groping for the charm bag, Steven could not take his eyes from Doryty, and was horrified to see she was no longer alone.

Around the old woman stood the shadowy figures of the drowned smugglers. They were dressed as they would have been on that fateful night, but the clothes they wore looked tattered and torn, as if they had been worn down over the years, as if the sea was still taking its toll. They were also wet, dripping wet, enough to pool into the sand around their bare feet.

*The Cursed Shore*

Doryty was standing shoulder to shoulder with one of the ghosts; the two of them looked so alike they could have been mother and daughter.

'Just keeping my kin company,' Doryty yelled back, and as if on cue, the ghostly woman beside her started to hum a now familiar tune.

The others joined in and the hum turned into a chant, rising louder and louder above the sound of the waves. Finally, Doryty added her voice to the chant and as soon as she did Steven felt the compulsion to hum the tune too, keeping perfect time with the ancient ghosts.

Trevan took advantage of the moment, he grabbed hold of Steven and groaned in his ear. 'What are you doing, you idiot? Why would you help the witch? We are on your side, stop this and I will prove it.'

His words scratched at Steven's brain trying to pry away at the wall he had built to protect himself from the truth. However, he could not stop now. He was committed. He had to follow Doryty's command, he had no choice and even if he could comprehend it, it was too late for reason now.

'What did you do to protect me?' he hissed back at Trevan, in a voice that was not his own.

Trevan hesitated, looking confused and Steven seized his chance and grabbed again at Trevan's neck, searching for the pouch. The two men continued to struggle clumsily with each other, for them both the pouch was life or death.

As Steven's searching fingers finally wrapped around the prize, he put all his weight into shouldering Trevan in the chest. Trevan lost his footing and stumbled backwards; as he did so the leather cord, which held the pouch, snapped. Steven seized his chance before Trevan could react and kicked out at the man, causing him to stagger back a few more paces, which left him standing in the shallow water.

Steven readied himself, expecting Trevan to run back at him but instead the police officer stood stock still as if unable to move. His eyes were wide open in terror and disbelief as he mumbled words, pleading for mercy Steven presumed, but he could not hear them, the now howling wind blew the words away before they reached his ears. He walked slowly towards the stricken man, ignoring the look of hope on his face and with a last kick to the stomach, Constable Andrew Trevan staggered back further into the foamy water. Trevan's face twisted in horror as he flailed about in panic and he stumbled and fell into the shallow waves.

Steven stumbled backwards himself as the tide suddenly rushed in. A rip current pushed the seawater further onto the beach and it stretched out like a hand to embrace the stricken police officer, pulling him away from the safety of the beach.

Trevan continued to struggle and screamed and tried to stand again but a second wave, higher this time, covered him and started to pull him out to sea. Steven stared in disbelief as ghostly hands appeared from the water and grabbed hold of the man, stopping him from swimming, keeping him down, drowning him.

As Trevan's writhing body disappeared beneath the water for the last time, the wind calmed, and the tide withdrew, taking its victim with it. The moon appeared once more from behind the clouds and everything on the beach appeared normal, as if something horrific had not just taken place. But it had. Constable Trevan was gone.

Despite the return to a mild summer's night Steven stood shivering, shocked at what he had caused to happen. He clutched his arms around himself and rocked slightly as he struggled to breathe. Had he just committed murder? The insanity that had taken hold of him began to drain away and as it dissipated, in rushed the full realisation of what he had done. He frantically stared at the endless blue of the sea hoping to see some sign of Trevan, he was ready to kick his shoes off and dive in to save the man, but Trevan was nowhere to be seen.

*The Cursed Shore*

Steven knew he would never be able to undo the horror he had committed. He had killed an innocent man because of an ancient atrocity; he had sent Andrew Trevan to his death to end a nightmare that no one would ever believe.

He walked back up the beach towards the car park his legs buckling under him, the leather pouch still clutched in his hand like a grim trophy. He tried to make sense of all the thoughts whirling around his head. Were the nightmares so bad that he had to resort to murder to end them? Was this really the only way? It had all been so obvious before but now the doubts were creeping in.

He had killed Trevan, but it needed to be done, by him or someone else; a Trevan had to die, Doryty said so. It wasn't even as if he held the man under the water, he just removed his charm pouch, and maybe kicked him in the right direction a bit. He tried not to think of Trevan's words, the sincere way he pleaded his innocence, as if he wasn't even aware of Steven's nightmares.

When he neared the car park, he came out of his stupor enough to remember that he wasn't alone. Doryty still stood at the foot of the cliff, next to the old mooring ring. Of course, she would be there, watching her dirty work done for her as Trevan had said. She smiled sweetly as he glowered at her.

'I do hope your little nightmares end now, dear,' she said kindly. 'You should be safe for a while at least.'

Steven stopped in his tracks as ice water began to flood through his veins.

'What do you mean for a while?'

His question was whispered but Doryty heard it clear enough and laughed like a child caught up to mischief once more, and Steven could only wonder at how he had ever found that laugh endearing.

'I'm surprised you never asked what the murders had to do with your nasty little dreams, dearie. Not much of an investigator are you, dear?' she said, echoing her earlier insult.

'Tell me then,' he mumbled through numbed lips.

Doryty smiled, a cold, evil, smile, she had clearly been waiting for this moment.

'Thought it was all about you didn't you, boy? So caught up in your own misery you were blind to the bigger picture. Like I said before, my sister, she tried to teach some young'uns to carry on after she went, your Sandra and her friends, but they didn't have the power. They knew the rites, knew how to sing the curse back to where it came from. They thought they could protect those that deserved to die, but without the power of a witch like Marjory, they might as well have been singing hymns in church. What were your sorry little dreams next to their mission? Even your own girlfriend knew you wasn't worth bothering with.'

Steven's heart lurch in his chest. Trevan, Sandra and the others, all on that clifftop, trying to protect the ancestors of the Revenue men, and he had thought they were evil. They hadn't been harming him. Nothing they did was anything to do with him, how had Doryty convinced him otherwise?

He had heard enough, he wanted to curl up on the sand and die, but Doryty hadn't finished with her gloating yet.

'Wasting their time, they were though. As I said before, you can't kill a curse, dearie. The best they could do was keep it at bay. You can't outrun a curse either, and tonight, thanks to you, a Trevan found that out. Tricky lot they are but I got one this time.'

Doryty gave another little laugh that finished Steven off as he sank to knees wishing the sand would swallow him up so he would never have to try to make sense of this madness. Doryty walked past him, giving him a little pat on the head as she left the beach.

'Don't forget, young Steven, your kin were there on that dreadful night too, chained to the mooring ring, waiting for the sea to take their lives. It was your kin that chanted the ancient words along with mine. Poured their souls into its meaning they did and helped give it its power. You know the right of it, 'tis in your blood, in your bones. You shared the same anger that I have and did what we needed to be done. Jacob is so proud of you. They all are.'

Steven looked passed her, of her ghostly conspirators only one remained. A tall man, a swathe of dark hair dripping its ghostly seawater down a familiar face, a face Steven saw in the mirror every morning. Jacob Pearn nodded to him as if in greeting, but Steven could only stare in horror at the apparition before him as it faded into the darkness.

*January 25th, 1796, Aglets Cove, Cornwall*

As Jacob Pearn succumbed to the sea, his mind full of Sarah Scadden's curse he thought once more of those he was leaving behind, his beloved wife and his beautiful sons. He would never hold them again or tell them how much he loved them. He hoped they would grow up strong and healthy. He hoped one day they or their kin would put things to right, avenge his death and make the Revenue pay the price for what they had done this night. Then, as everything faded to black, Jacob felt the warmth of Sarah Scadden's hand on his. He had thought the witch already dead, but the hand that found his was alive and comforting. She gave it a little squeeze which despite everything, gave him hope.

Then he knew no more.

# CHAPTER 29

Steven did not remember falling asleep that night or even what happened after got home. He awoke shivering in the morning, curled up on the kitchen floor of his cottage. There was an empty bottle of brandy beside him. Had it been full before? He couldn't remember that either.

He managed to struggle to a sitting position and waited for the room to catch up to him. Unbidden, the memories of last night came crushing down on him and he put his head in his hands and wept.

That was how Sandra found him. He hadn't even shut the door when he came in and she had ambled in as bright as a summer's morning to find him, totally wrecked on the kitchen floor. 'Come on now, Steven. You have to pull yourself together,' she said sitting down next to him. 'We don't have time for you to wallow in self-pity over another nightmare.'

Steven looked up sharply intensifying the room's steady circle of his head.

'Why are you here?' he mumbled through thick lips and a mouth that was refusing to cooperate. 'Do you know what I've done? You will hate me when you know.'

Steven held on to Sandra as if clinging on to sanity itself as he recounted the previous night's events. Sandra sat and listened wide-eyed and trembling, and Steven admired her attempt not to cry as the tears welled in her eyes.

Eventually, her resolve broke and the two of them sat sobbing on the kitchen floor, holding onto each other. In time, the tears stopped, and Steven was numb again,

*Ellen Hiller*

absence of any kind of feeling, a flatness of the world around him that he didn't have a right to be a part of anymore.

Sandra sighed and wiped her eyes. It was the sort of forced sigh that acknowledged even though he had killed one of her dear friends and pretty much destroyed their chances to save other potential victims of the curse, he too was a victim.

'I'll put some coffee on.' She didn't say it benevolently, or lovingly, Sandra was being brisk and efficient, and Steven welcomed it.

The room had slowed its spinning to a less nauseous level, but Steven thought it unwise to move just yet, so he sat there on the floor watching her potter about in the small kitchen. When she was done, Sandra sat back on the floor beside him and handed him the comfortingly warm mug.

'I'm sorry,' he said after a while, fresh tears welling in his eyes, this time though they were not for himself.

Sandra put her hand on his to comfort him, but he quickly pulled away.

'I'm sorry,' he explained. 'Doryty used to do that all the time.'

'It's okay,' she said, understanding. 'Doryty used you, you didn't know her, and she used your ignorance to dupe you. She is a powerful witch; more powerful than even Marjory was. You didn't stand a chance of resisting her.'

'I don't remember her doing anything witch-like to me though, she was just like a sweet old grandmother who cared about me,' Steven said.

Sandra sniffed and said, 'The best magic is the magic you don't see, or the magic you only think you see.' Steven nodded.

'Why did the sisters live together if they were such enemies?' he asked.

'I don't think they were enemies as such,' Sandra said. 'Just two old witches with very different opinions. They were sisters too, remember, never underestimate that bond.'

'So, Marjory was like a white witch and Doryty is a black one?'

Sandra winced at his naivety. 'There is no such thing as black magic or white magic, Steven. There is only magic,' she tried to explain. 'There is chaos magic though, but that's a whole other chapter. Doryty doesn't use it, she just uses the power she has for what she believes to be the right reasons, but they are not reasons that any normal person would agree with.'

'I see,' Steven said as convincingly as he could. 'And you are a witch too then, but you use your power for the right reasons I suppose.'

Sandra sighed and ran her fingers through her hair.

'Firstly,' she said, 'I'm not sure I actually have any powers as such. Marjory said she saw something in me that could be coaxed out, but I think I am just good at following instructions. Most of what we do is ritual stuff that's not a lot different to following a recipe in a cookbook. And yes, I do see what I do as for the right reasons. I protect people, Steven, I don't harm them.'

Steven tried not to take it as a personal rebuke, but he wasn't done with the guilt trip yet.

'I see,' he repeated meekly.

The coffee was finished now but still Steven did not want to move. He did not want to be a part of this crazy new world that he found himself in. He wished there was a rabbit hole he could climb out of to make everything return to normal. Sandra seemed to instinctively know how he felt, or maybe she had more power than she had given herself credit for. 'The curse still needs to be held at bay,' she said, reaching for his hand. 'I can't do it alone, Steven.'

Steven looked into her eyes, an ember of redemption beginning to glow inside of him. 'You mean I could help, even after everything I've done?'

'Sure, I can teach you what you need to know, at least as much as you will need to be useful. I have a feeling there is something of the craft in you, Steven. Doryty must have always known that and used it against you, used your own power to make hers stronger.'

The ember grew brighter. 'Maybe it could go some way towards putting right what I did?' he asked hopefully.

'Maybe,' Sandra smiled; though it lacked sincerity, Steven was still grateful for it.

'I still have Marjory's journals,' she told him, 'and there are others who know what is going on and who can help in their own little ways. It's possible we can find another other four needed for the ritual.'

Steven's raised an eyebrow and smirked. 'Is there anyone in this village that isn't in on this?' he asked.

Sandra laughed but did not answer. Even so, that ember of hope was glowing brightly within him now, and Steven welcomed the warmth of it as it began to flow through his body and push away the numbness. Of course, it could have been the coffee, but he put that thought aside. He had a new sense of purpose to replace his feelings of self-hatred and he clung to it like a piece of driftwood in a stormy sea.

'But first there is the problem of Doryty,' Sandra said, and Steven's heart sank again on hearing the witches name once more. 'We have to break her hold over you, because believe me, whatever she is using she can still use, even if you know what she is up to this time. Think back to the time you spent with her, was there anything strange or unusual that she said or did?'

Steven thought for a while. 'She did squeeze my hand a lot, I found it very reassuring.'

*The Cursed Shore*

'I'm sure you did,' Sandra said, 'but I'm thinking it would have to have been something more physical, like Andrew's charm pouch.'

The words tore at him and he sank down into himself once more, crushed by the memory. He had taken away the man's last protection. Sandra reached over again and this time he let her hold him.

'It wasn't you; it was Doryty,' she said reassuringly. 'Hold on to that thought. The hag programmed you, manipulated you, she sent you the nightmares until your reason was lost.'

Steven sat up straight again and stared at her. 'Did you always know it was her sending me the nightmares? Why didn't you tell me before?'

Sandra looked down and fiddled with her empty mug. 'I wasn't sure. It could have just been your connection to Jacob. I thought with Marjory gone maybe the curse was reaching out through him to you. I admit I never took your nightmares seriously enough. I am so sorry, Steven, if I had, things might have turned out differently. In my defence, Marjory had died and left it to us to hold the curse at bay. We were failing badly and trying to fix it took all of my focus.'

Steven nodded. 'The bodies on the beach,' he said.

Sandra lowered her head and nodded.

'When we started working with Marjory the only deaths on the beach were historical ones. We did the ritual with her but I'm not sure any of us really understood how important it was. Then she died and the first body washed up a few days later. We had failed. After that, we were terrified of the responsibility and the bodies kept on coming. I guess we were so caught up in our own mission I didn't see how dangerous the connection with you was.'

Steven nodded and closed his eyes. He could see all the pieces beginning to fit together now. 'With Marjory gone,' he said. 'Doryty saw her chance to let the curse run on forever. She knew she could get rid of the rest of you, but she needed me to kill Andrew Trevan. He was too well protected for her to touch. I was a convenient tool.'

'And your connection to Jacob Pearn, Steven, was too much for her to resist.'

Seeing how lost Steven was, Sandra snaked her arms around him and lay her head on his shoulder. They sat on the floor of the kitchen hugging each other and Steven didn't want the moment to end; here was comfort and forgiveness but when it stopped, there would be the harsh slap of the reality that he had to face once more.

A loud bang on the front door interrupted his thoughts. No doubt, the police had come for him. The bang was followed by a crash as the front door swung inwards and loosely, hanging on by one hinge. In the doorway stood a very wet but very alive Andrew Trevan.

Sandra screamed with joy then ran across the kitchen, throwing herself on to the half-downed man, kissing and hugging him, crying, and thanking her gods that he was alive.

Over her shoulder, Trevan glared at Steven, but Steven didn't care. Overwhelmed with relief, he fought the urge to run and hug and kiss the man himself. He wondered if the relief he felt was because Andrew wasn't dead after all or, more selfishly, if it was because that fact meant he was no longer a murderer. Fate had dealt him a kind blow this time. He was off the hook, sort of. He still had to explain his actions to Trevan and hope for forgiveness. However, for now, all he could do was to mumble through trembling lips: 'You're alive, I can't believe you're alive,' as Trevan, with Sandra still attached walked towards him.

Steven pulled himself to his feet and readied himself for the pounding he knew he deserved. He didn't care if Trevan chose to beat him to death or arrest him, nothing could make him feel bad right now. He was so deliriously happy he could almost see rainbows, fireworks, and dancing unicorns.

*The Cursed Shore*

The punch never came, however, nor the handcuffs and the reading of his rights.

'You got a towel or what?' Trevan asked. The blandness of his question knocked Steven from his revelry. Sandra ran off to the bathroom to fetch towels.

'You broke my door,' Steven heard himself say.

Andrew Trevan raised an eyebrow then laughed.

'Sorry about that,' he said, 'I was in a hurry. I saw Sandra's car outside and thought she might be in danger.'

Steven nodded and studied his feet for a while. The whole enormity of the situation was sinking in and finally everything was beginning to make sense to Steven.

'I'm so sorry Andrew, how could I have got everything so wrong?'

'Wasn't your fault, mate,' Trevan graciously admitted as he took the towel from Sandra and started patting himself down with it. 'Doryty is a powerful witch. She must have had you enthralled under some powerful magic. I should have seen the signs, I thought she might just be using you to spy on us, but to make you do something like that there had to be magic involved. Do me a favour and second guess everything you feel compelled to do till we sort it.'

Steven nodded vigorously. 'But how did you survive?' Steven asked, perplexed. 'I saw you get swept away.'

'Aye and with quite a speed too. Luckily, I had my wits about me, and maybe a little help from the gods. Oh, and this in my pocket.'

Andrew held out his hand and showed them the pouch he had made for Sandra. 'I managed to get my hand in there and touch it,' he explained. 'Soon as I did, the spell released me, and I surfaced just outside the cove. I swam back in farther along the shore.'

'Thank the gods,' Sandra proclaimed again. She took the pouch from Trevan's outstretched hands then handed it straight back again. 'You keep it; make me another one,

*Ellen Hiller*

that one's all wet.' Steven snorted a laugh. Nothing phased that woman, he thought. Practical to the last.

'Come on, let's get you cleaned up too,' Sandra said, and dragged Steven towards the stairs. 'Go up and have a shower, and while you are in there, keep thinking about your meetings with Doryty. And throw some clean clothes down for Andrew; you look about the same size.'

Steven obeyed, calling over his shoulder as he wobbled up the stairs. 'We did drink a lot of tea at Doryty's, and there was always cake.'

'Keep thinking,' Sandra called back.

Steven was glad she hadn't thought it was the cake. He would miss the cake.

As he showered, Steven clung to Sandra's words. The thought of being able to do something positive to undo the harm he had done, as well as having her and Trevan understand him at last had erased the last of the guilt he had been feeling. If only Sandra and Andrew hadn't been so secretive before, but then would he have believed them with Doryty whispering in his ear? Probably not. He thought back to his visits to Doryty's cottage but came up with nothing.

The thought of Doryty sitting on her chair in that strange room sent shivers down Steven's spine. She could be plotting anything, including his own death. He stood there letting the water pool over his head; he didn't notice it. Of course, he realised, Doryty would kill him, Sandra too. She would presume that Sandra was the last witch left of Marjory's coven and now that he had fulfilled his purpose, he was a dangerous witness. Not that anyone would believe his story if he told it.

That left one thing that had to be done. He had believed he could kill Trevan to save them, so he guessed he could kill someone again if it was necessary, and this one truly was evil. He would have to live with the guilt, because Doryty had to die.

# CHAPTER 30

It was 1 a.m. and the whole of Aglets Cove appeared to be asleep except for himself and Sandra. They had left Andrew to return home. The man was exhausted, and an exhausted Andrew was no good to anyone.

Every small sound they made was a cacophony in his ears that was sure to wake everyone up. 'I'm still not sure we should be doing this,' Sandra whispered as they crouched under Doryty's window, 'and I know it wouldn't have been fair to involve Andrew in this bit, but I wish he was here instead of me.'

'Shh!' he whispered back, then he added in what he believed was a more appropriate, quieter whisper, 'Well we have to do it, we are as good as dead if we don't, and I've done enough to Andrew without risking his career on top of trying to kill him. Anyway, if we fail there needs to be someone else to try to stop her.'

He shared Sandra's apprehension, but he knew this had to be done if there was ever going to be an end to his suffering, or a way to stop the curse. He was done with being manipulated, he was done with the nightmares and he was done with Doryty.

Sandra nodded solemnly and handed him the crowbar. Jimmying the window was easier than he had expected and not half as noisy either and they were soon climbing over the ledge and stepping through the open window.

Despite all that Doryty had done to him, he still felt terrible standing in the strange little room uninvited. As far as he could tell in the gloom, everything seemed as it was before, nothing stranger or more sinister but he knew he shouldn't be there. All was deathly quiet, yet he was sure they were being watched.

'Be careful of the cat, it might make a noise if we startle it,' Steven whispered.

'I didn't know Doryty had a cat,' Sandra whispered back. 'Almost makes her seem nicer.'

'Yeah, little calico one. Persistent little thing, it kind of grew on me. I'm going to take it with me when we are done.'

'Marjory had a little calico cat,' she whispered in his ear. 'It died a few days before she did.'

Steven froze. For all the hours Steven had spent in this place with the little calico cat perched on his lap, Doryty had never once acknowledged its existence. Maybe, just maybe, no that was ridiculous. Was it a ghost cat? Maybe it was part of the spell. He whispered his thoughts to Sandra who stood staring at him blank faced, eyes blinking rapidly as she digested this new information. Then she smiled.

'Did the cat ever try to draw your attention to anything or distract you from something?' Sandra asked.

Steven thought back and remembered the time he had been looking around the shelves when Doryty was in the kitchen. The cat had jumped on one of the shelves, and in the knocking over of the bottles revealed the little figure of a man. He darted as quickly and as quietly as he could over to the shelf in question, reached over the bottles at the front and pulled out the figure. Sandra immediately grabbed it and pointed to the window. Steven shook his head and gestured towards the stairs. Sandra shook her head adamantly and proceeded to climb out of the window. Steven had no choice and followed her.

Although he had his mind set on killing the old witch, he couldn't help but be relieved at not having to do so. Not yet anyway. Once he was outside, Steven eased the window down again and ran after Sandra who was already

*The Cursed Shore*

out of the garden and standing in the lane. He was breathless when he caught up with her.

'I take it this is the source of my misery then,' he said, nodding at the effigy in her hand.

'Yes, that must be one of your hairs wrapped around it. I wonder how she got it?' Sandra replied.

The memory hit Steven like a sledgehammer. The funeral procession on the morning he first arrived in the village, it seemed like a lifetime ago now. The tug of his hair when her ring was caught, or so he had thought at the time.

'Bitch!' he snarled through gritted teeth. That's when she started this, before he even knew her. She must have known about his family connection to Jacob and planned this from the very start. Bile rose in his throat as more possible pieces of the puzzle forced their way into his brain. What if this went back further than that? He had only moved back to Cornwall because he had inherited his grandmother's cottage. Was her death a natural one, or was it a convenient one? His parents would have inherited the cottage if they were alive. Did Doryty cause the car crash that had killed them just as she had caused Penny's?

Sandra had to grab him to stop him from running back down the lane to finish the job and kill the old witch.

'We have to dispose of this first,' she said. 'She could still be linked to it even if it's no longer in her possession, and it could even have power over you after her death. We have to destroy it before we destroy her.'

Steven calmed down and bowed to her wisdom.

'And how do we do that?'

'Phone Andrew and tell him to meet us at my place. Then you get to see us doing witchy stuff. I know there is a spell that will break this in Marjory's book of shadows.'

'book of shadows sounds a bit spooky,' he said

Sandra smiled at him. 'It's just like a witch's cookbook and diary really, nothing spooky about it at all. All witches have their own but Marjory passed hers on to me before she died. She must have known I would need it, bless her.'

They had reached his car now and climbed in to begin the silent drive to Sandra's cottage. They were both too wrapped up in their own thoughts for idle chitchat. Steven was pleased that he would see the effigy destroyed. He wanted to thank the cat and give it a big hug. Was it a ghost cat? Surely not, it had been too solid, too prickly, and it moulted hairs everywhere. Then the thought occurred to him: there could have been two cats, one for each sister. With all that had happened over the last few weeks, he still tried to cling to the beliefs he used to have when life was normal. There was safety back when witches and curses were something you watched on Netflix at Halloween.

# CHAPTER 31

Steven sat on Sandra's sofa chatting to a now dry but crumpled Andrew. He guessed the man had crashed out on the sofa when he got home. Steven didn't blame him. He knew himself how exhausting fighting for your life was, real or imagined.

Both men watched as Sandra set out the elements of their craft. It was clearly something she was well-practised in, a part of her life that he could never have imagined. She drew a large circle on the floor with salt and sat inside, then beckoned him and Andrew to do the same. She then lit small candles and set them out in another, smaller, circle, laying the effigy of Steven in the middle. After this, she took an old jar from a box, containing what looked like a mixture of dried herbs and salt and dirt. This Sandra sprinkled over the figure as she read strange words she had copied down from Marjory's book.

Finally, she slowly unwound the long dark hair from the effigy and returned it to Steven. He had no idea what to do with it so unceremoniously stuffed it into his pocket. Sandra cleaned up the mess she had made and threw the doll in the bin.

'Is that it?' he asked.

'Yup.'

'I thought I would feel something,' he said.

'Maybe you will after a good night's sleep,' she said.

The thought of it sent a thrill through him and he couldn't hold back the grin. He was all excited like a child on Christmas Eve, full of the anticipation of the night-time and Santa's visit. He could see himself in his bed,

*Ellen Hiller*

snuggled in the oversized duvet, closing his eyes, and knowing that the nightmare would not come. Tonight, he knew would not drown. He would sleep.

Steven's shoulders slumped, and he exhaled a long lingering breath as the tension he had been holding on to for so long left his body. Sandra smiled and winked at him.

'Feeling it now?' she asked. He chuckled and shook his head in disbelief.

'What happens next?' he asked, though what he wanted to say 'was can I go to bed now?'

'What do you think happens next?' she answered and anticipating his answer added, 'and no, you can't go to bed yet.'

With a slow realisation, the grin slid from Steven's face.

'We still have to kill her, don't we?'

Sandra nodded solemnly.

'We must do it before she notices the effigy is missing or she'll come for us first. It's not just about us, either. She is a powerful witch; she can undo everything we try to do. While she lives, we have no hope of stopping the curse.'

'Sounds familiar,' Steven said. 'I can remember Doryty saying something similar about Andrew,' he said sheepishly and for a moment, he thought that Sandra was going to slap him, but he underestimated her patience.

She took a deep breath. 'I know how strange all this must be to you, you were kind of thrown in the deep end wasn't you? But I really need you to trust me.' Steven nodded his affirmation, he wanted to add the bit where Doryty had told him there was no stopping the curse but didn't think Doryty's words of wisdom would go down very well right now. Then a thought occurred to him.

'Does Doryty have a coven? Is she passing on her knowledge before she dies, like Marjory did?'

'Not that I know of,' Sandra answered. But the sudden tension in her face revealed her uncertainty. 'I can't imagine anyone else has a vested interest in the curse.'

*The Cursed Shore*

Steven nodded, it sounded reasonable and with four curse victims in such a short amount of time it seemed she was probably going all out for revenge before she died of old age.

'Let's hope so,' he agreed. He stood up and stretched, 'So are we going back to her cottage to kill her as planned, a pillow over her face as she sleeps?' Steven thought that killing her in her sleep had a certain justice about it.

'Ugh, no details please!' Andrew looked horrified. 'Plausible deniability, remember?'

'Sorry mate, pretend you didn't hear that,' Steven said.

Andrew gave him a wry look and continued, 'Like that would have worked anyway, you seem to be forgetting the bit where she is a powerful and vengeful witch.'

'Oh yeah, that bit,' Sandra said pulling a face, guess we wasn't thinking straight. 'So how do we kill her then?'

'Go and get Marjory's book, Sandra,' Steven said. 'There must be something in there to cover it.'

Steven doubted that Marjory would have a chapter on how to kill one's sibling, but he was curious to see the famous book.

While Sandra went to find the book, Steven looked at Andrew and awkwardly, he thought of something random to say to break the silence, but nothing seemed adequate. Andrew saved him the trouble.

'So, Steven, while we are waiting, I'd love to hear about things from Doryty's point of view. It's hard to believe how you fell in with the bitter old woman, my arch enemy, if you like. I bet she had a few choice words to say about me.'

Steven realised that it was those words Andrew wanted to hear most of all. Andrew wanted to know if Doryty saw him as a challenge, or simply mocked his ineptitude. He thought back to the conversations they had had together sitting on those too comfy chairs whilst sipping tea.

*Ellen Hiller*

'She called you a cunning man once,' he remembered. 'I didn't think it was a particularly insulting thing to say, maybe it was to her.'

Andrew laughed. 'She wasn't calling me names, mate; she was describing me. A cunning man is another way of saying male witch. It's an old English term.'

'Well that conversation might have gone a little differently if I'd known,' Steven said.

Andrew nodded. 'Guess we have a lot to teach you.'

'Yeah, like everything,' Steven answered, wondering how much of it he could look up on Google first, so he didn't seem so naïve.

'Just don't ask the internet,' Andrew continued, and Steven wondered if cunning men could also read minds. 'Too many fairy stories mingled with half-truths to gain any useful insights there,' he concluded.

'It's okay,' Steven said. 'Thought never entered my head.'

Sandra saved Steven from any more social awkwardness by appearing in the doorway with the impressive tome. She handed it to Steven. It was everything a witch's book should be: huge and leather bound, with big brass hinges and a jewelled clasp. There was a pentagram embossed on the front, but there was no title. With great reverence, Steven opened the book and began turning the thick parchment pages.

The book of shadows was full of handwritten notes and drawings of flowers and herbs. There were strange symbols with their meanings scrawled at the side, recipes for potions and medicines, and of course, spells. It was magnificent.

He came to a stop when he reached the centre of the book; here she had drawn a sort of family tree in tiny writing that covered the two pages. He held the book closer trying to make sense of it and Andrew leaned over his shoulder, interested. The connections did not make sense. When he had traced his own family tree online,

*The Cursed Shore*

there had been a clear connection following the male linage of his family. This one was all higgledy-piggledy following both female and male offspring as far back as the 17$^{th}$ century.

'Must be the historical linage of the Scadden witches,' Andrew said. 'Stops well before Doryty and Marjory were born though. Wonder why?'

'No more room,' shrugged Steven. 'Sarah Scadden must be here though,' and he followed the line from the top again until he found her. There was a noisy intake of breath at the side of him as Andrew read over his shoulder.

'Sandra, come have a look at this,' Andrew said with a slight tremble in his voice.

She looked to where he was pointing in the book and noted 'Oh, Sarah Scadden had three sisters and a brother.' Andrew moved his finger lower to uncover the next line. 'And they in turn married…' Then she saw it. The youngest was married to Jacob Pearn.

'You're a Scadden as well as a Pearn!' She almost screamed it and Steven slammed the book shut and threw it on the coffee table as if he could distance himself from this new connection.

He noticed Andrew was chuckling to himself then the man yelled 'Yes!', punched the air and gave Steven a huge bear hug. Steven looked at Sandra and even she seemed bemused.

'Don't you two see?' Andrew asked. 'We have a Scadden witch!'

'Yes, I think we got that bit,' Sandra replied. Andrew continued.

'There has always been a Scadden witch to stop the curse, until Marjory died and Doryty went native, then it all went to shit.'

'Oh,' Sandra and Steven said in unison the penny finally beginning to drop.

'So, if I take part in the ritual, people will stop dying?' Steven asked.

*Ellen Hiller*

'I'm sure of it,' Andrew replied. 'But we still have to stop Doryty. Like as not she knows this, has always known it. Sandra always thought you had something of the craft about you that Doryty was using. Even with the effigy destroyed she might still try to control you via the connection of blood.'

'Okay, let's get back on it,' said Steven as he reached out to grab the book back off the coffee table, but he stopped halfway and sat back sharply.

'Do you see it?' he hissed through clenched teeth.

'See what?' Sandra asked, looking around the room.

'The cat's sitting in front of the table.'

Sandra peered at the spot Steven indicated but could see nothing.

'Cat?' was all Andrew managed to say. The little calico cat jumped onto the table and then, just like every cat in existence, mortal or apparently otherwise, it subtly stretched out a paw and knocked the book onto the floor.

Sandra squealed and jumped back a few paces while Andrew sat back sharply and gasped.

'The cat did it,' Steven said and Andrew looked at him with a confused expression. Sandra quickly got him up to speed regarding the cat whilst screwing up her eyes and peering across the table still trying to see it.

'The ghost of Marjory's cat,' she said.

'Or Marjory as the ghost of her cat,' Steven said.

Sandra scowled at him. 'If the cat is Marjory then why can't we see it? We should be able to see it too.'

Steven was about to give a smug reply when he realised the cat was playing with the fallen book and clawing at something that was protruding from the spine. He reached over, pulled a piece of paper out, and gave the cat a stroke and a tickle under the chin as he did so.

'That looked weird,' Sandra said, and Steven wondered if Doryty had ever thought the same about his interactions with the cat in her cottage.

Steven carefully unrolled the small piece of paper he had pulled from the book and read the brutally honest title.

'How to kill Doryty.'

'Perfect! But why did she hide it so well?' Sandra asked.

'I don't know,' replied Steven, 'but the cat's looking sheepish.'

'The ghost cat must have always been part of Marjory's plan,' Andrew said. 'After all, she wouldn't have wanted Doryty to find that piece of information by chance.'

Steven and Sandra agreed, and together they studied the instructions.

# CHAPTER 32

Unlike the book of shadows, the instructions for killing Doryty were written on modern lined paper in a clear steady hand, quite unlike the chaotic scrawling in the old tome. It was obvious that this had been written recently and with the intention that others would be reading it, and that no mistakes or misunderstandings could be made.

Sandra read the instructions aloud.

'If you are reading this my work has failed and Doryty is empowering the curse. I am truly sorry that it has come to this, but you must be brave, my dears, and follow my instructions. You will know by now that I have sent a little friend to guide you. This will have taken the last of my power, but it is all I can do to try to support you. I have put a little of myself into my dear little Cleo. I hope it is enough. Some may see it some may not. I expect Doryty will be aware of it, but she is unlikely to know its purpose or be able to do anything about it. I outrank her even in death. Now to business.'

Steven grinned at Sandra and Andrew. 'So if I can see it and you can't, I must be a better witch than you amateurs.'

Sandra did not even bother responding to that one and merely shook her head.

'Thank the gods you happened along then,' Andrew said. 'Someone obviously needed to see the cat, I don't want to think what would have happened if there was no one who could.'

'From what I've heard about Marjory I don't think she would have left something this important to chance,' said

*The Cursed Shore*

Steven, 'and anyway, even if you didn't have me to see the cat you would have still seen the book fly off the table.'

'Yeah that's true,' Andrew agreed sounding relieved. Sandra continued reading out the message.

'Doryty sleeps very deeply so the middle of the night will be the time to do it. However, despite her deep sleep she will be aware of you as soon as you are in close proximity to her.'

Sandra looked up at this and pulled an oops face at Steven. It seemed they had gotten lucky in finding the effigy without disturbing her, it could all have gone horribly wrong. Sandra continued.

'When you are close, act fast. Someone must hold her hands still while another places a sliver of mandrake into her mouth. After that, work quickly to bind her hands together and cut out her tongue. After this, she will not be able to speak a spell or weave one. Do not hesitate or think about what you are doing, or you will falter, and she will overpower you. Your actions must be swift and sure.'

'Her own sister,' Steven whispered under his breath.

'After she is muted, check her body, all of it, for any amulets or charms, when you have done that, read the spell I have written at the bottom of this letter. This will dismantle any protection spells helping her. After this, she is yours to do with as you wish. Do not fail. If it has come to this, there must be no room in your hearts for pity. Always remember that it is not just your lives that are at risk if she survives.'

Sandra stopped briefly and thought of Penny and Mike, tears streamed down her face.

'Here, Sandra,' Andrew said softly, and took the piece of paper from her.

In a voice choked with emotion, Andrew read the last part.

'I love you all, please carry on the fight. It will never stop so long as a descendant of the Revenue men still lives. You must ensure that there is always someone to put up the barrier, to reflect the curse, until that time comes. With you always, Marjory.'

They sat there in silence for a while, letting Marjory's words sink in.

'So how do we do the final deed?' Steven eventually said. 'Smother her with her pillow, like we originally planned?'

'We could, but…' Sandra hesitated for a while. 'But I have something more fitting in mind. You are going to think I'm a monster though.'

# CHAPTER 33

Steven thought Sandra was a monster, enough to make him feel better about the monster he had become himself so that was a good thing, he told himself firmly.

As they crept into the bedroom Steven put the gym bag gently down beside the bed. Doryty continued to snore loudly. He briefly looked around the room. It was surprising how different it was from the room downstairs. Up here, everything was all crochet doilies and floral prints. It looked lived in and homely, just as he would have expected an old ladies' bedroom to be, not unlike Nan's room he thought then cursed himself for still thinking like that.

The door creaked slightly and both he and Sandra spun round to look. The small calico cat stood there watching them. 'Do you see it?' he whispered in Sandra's ear.

'See what?' she whispered back.

'The cat, it's here, it's watching us.' He saw the tension leave Sandra immediately.

'I wish I could,' she whispered. 'Marjory is watching over us. If I had any doubts before they are gone now.'

Just as well, thought Steven, eyeing the contents of the gym bag.

The room had grown quiet. Doryty had stopped snoring. Steven's heart almost exploded in his chest as he turned to see her watching them.

Sandra reacted first.

'Quick! Grab her hands!' Steven did not hesitate, not caring how much force he was using as he held her fast. Doryty screamed, and as she did so Sandra pushed the sliver of mandrake root into Doryty's mouth and held it closed. Doryty buckled and struggled with more strength than a grown man. Steven was freaked out as he fought to keep her under control, but he held on firmly.

Sandra reached into the gym bag with her free hand and came back with a pair of secateurs. She did not give pause of thought, as he knew he would have done; her actions were firm and decisive just as Marjory had instructed.

Steven felt a huge swell of pride and admiration for her as she reached into Doryty's mouth and pulled out her tongue, grasping it firmly with the nails on her thumb and forefinger, enough to draw blood. She pulled on it until Steven thought it would rip out of its own accord, then with one loud snip of the secateurs the tongue was cut through and the bloody lump of meat plopped onto the old woman's white nightdress. Doryty threw her head back and howled in pain, and Steven hated himself for pitying her.

'Sit her up now,' Sandra said. 'I don't want her to choke on the blood.'

Steven pulled on Doryty's hands until she was upright, and her head lolled forward. She was easier to manage now, and although she hissed and squeaked in pain and hatred, she was unable to speak a spell. The usually neat and tidy bun had come loose, her grey hair hanging wild and matted. Gibberish grunts came from her mouth that was drooling thick globs of blood down her chin. Her entire face contorted in pain.

How could this pathetic wretch have caused him so much misery? Why did she have to do it all, he wondered. She had been like a grandmother to him. He let go of her wrist and reached out to brush the hair from her face, to comfort her. Sandra jabbed him hard in his ribs and brought him back to reality. He quickly caught Doryty's wrist again just as she started to make an elaborate sign in the air. Dammit, she was still controlling him.

*The Cursed Shore*

Sandra rummaged in the bag again, this time bringing out a pair of handcuffs. Steven raised an eyebrow.

'Andrew's?' he asked, and she blushed slightly as she shook her head.

Together they pulled Doryty's arms behind her back and Sandra clipped the cuffs onto her wrists and tightened them. Now the witch could neither speak a spell nor weave one with her hands. They both relaxed slightly. She was subdued.

'Now we have to check her for amulet,' Steven said. 'Could you do that bit too, Sandra? It seems too, you know, personal.'

Sandra understood without further explanation and started tugging at Doryty's nightdress as Steven politely looked out of the window. He could watch her tongue being cut out and help to handcuff her but witnessing an old lady's dignity being transgressed was just too much for him.

Doryty continued to snarl and hiss and Steven heard the secateurs cut through something.

'Got it!' Sandra announced triumphantly. 'She had a carved sigil tied round her waist.'

Steven turned to look at it as Sandra pulled Doryty's nightgown back in place. The sigil was a round wooden disk with wavy carved lines and dots, not unlike one of the marks Steven had found carved into the ground at the bonfire site.

'That's everything then,' said Steven, 'ready for the next bit?'

'Absolutely,' said Sandra. 'Mind you don't get her blood all over you as you carry her downstairs and into the car.' Steven smiled, practical to the last he thought as Sandra stuffed a crochet doily in the old woman's mouth. 'Just in case,' she said.

They half carried and half pulled the struggling old lady down the stairs and into the quiet lane. Steven wondered if the neighbours would see them. It was unlikely at 3 a.m.

and if they did, would they even care? Did everyone in the village know about Doryty? Or had she fooled them with her sweet little old lady ruse, as she had him.

Nobody came out to stop them. There was not even the twitch of a curtain. How could it be so easy to do this to someone?

Once Doryty had been safely dumped in the boot of the car, Steven quickly drove to the beach. The tide would soon be on the turn. They would have to hurry before it started making its way back into the cove.

Doryty's eyes were bulging, her breath coming in short gasps as she struggled anew in the arms of Sandra and Steven as they carried her from the car park and onto the beach. It was clear the old woman knew what was coming, and the pitiful squawks coming from her blood-filled mouth was severely testing Steven's resolve.

Steven looked at her, trying not to find something of the loveable old grandmother left. She glared back at him with a face full of twisted malice and hate, she spat out the doily then spat globules of congealed blood in his face. It was all he needed to carry on. He could almost thank her for it as he lifted her higher in order to wipe the bloody mess on her nightdress.

They half carried, half dragged Doryty along the beach until they reached the rusty mooring ring set in the cliff. Sandra handed Steven a length of chain, he reached towards the ring and shuddered and hesitated, not daring to touch it.

'What if it still has an effect on me?' he said. Sandra nodded and took the chain from him.

'Best not chance it,' she agreed. Then, leaving Steven to manage Doryty, she looped the metal chain through the ring then back through the handcuffs and secured it in place with a padlock.

Doryty stood there trembling, her eyes black circles in her ashen face. She was unable to curse or plead. Chained to the mooring ring, just as her ancestor had been so many

*The Cursed Shore*

years before. With her powers muted, all she could do was stare and gasp at the sea as it crept further into the cove.

Steven took a moment to savour the great surge of elation and freedom that broke over him like a wave crashing over one of the rocks in the cove. It was done.

'Shall we go, Sandra?' he said.

'Yeah, I don't need to see this,' she replied.

With arms around each other they left the beach, heads touching as they murmured loving words to each other. To anyone watching they would have looked like any other romantic couple strolling along the moonlit beach.

And the tide rolled in.

# CHAPTER 34

The next morning another body was found on the beach; it was an old woman, as yet to be identified. According to Steven's editor, it looked like the tide had washed it in, just like the others. Steven wondered what happened to the handcuffs and chain, and he asked if there was any sign of a struggle, maybe visible bruising around the wrists.

'Apparently not,' said John, 'according to PC Trevan it must have been in the water for some time, enough to lose any useful evidence. The tongue was missing, presumed eaten by wildlife, and that was all.'

'Another accidental death then,' Steven said.

'Yep, seems so,' John answered, 'According to Trevan the poor old dear must have slipped off the cliff path in the dark.'

Steven nodded knowingly, and John winked back at him but nothing more was said. Steven had so many questions; this time however, he would be asking Andrew and Sandra. How different things would have been if they had been open with him from the start. Would he have believed them though, he wondered? Probably not.

The next night, after a blissful dreamless sleep, Steven joined Sandra and Andrew at the bonfire site. The wood was piled high, and the sigils carved deep into the earth.

'Will we be able to do it with just the three of us?' Steven asked as Sandra lit the fire. She smiled up at him, then past him. Steven turned to see John, his editor, walking along the cliff path, dressed as he was in a long black hooded robe. Behind him strode Paul Smith the

*The Cursed Shore*

pathologist and Seargent Wheeler the scene of crimes officer. Steven laughed out loud.

'Of course,' he said. 'Is there anyone in this place not involved?' he asked as two more people strolled along the path to the site.

Sandra didn't answer, she just linked arms with him and together they sang the strange words that she had taught him, the same words that Jacob Pearn and his fellow smugglers had sung as they died. It was an echo of the ghostly sounds that now came up from the beach below. A wall for the curse to hit and rebound, sending it back from where it had come from. Steven hoped it would be enough, that this time it would work. Andrew, at least, was smiling confidently. Encouraged by this Steven poured his heart and soul into the chant the way his ancestor had done all those years ago. Would it be enough? He guessed tomorrow the tide would let them know.

As they all stood around the bonfire, their new enthusiasm burning brighter than the flames, Steven noticed the little calico cat sitting at his feet and he was comforted by its presence. What he didn't see, a little way behind him, darker than the dancing shadows cast by the fire, was the hideous figure of an old woman. It hissed quietly from the gaping wound of a mouth that dripped oily black blood onto her dripping wet nightdress. Slowly, ever so slowly, she reached out a clawed hand, dripping with seawater, towards him.

The cat turned and hissed back at the woman who flinched and slowly withdrew her hand again before taking a step back, retreating even deeper into the shadows.

The End

*Ellen Hiller*